THE HUNTER

Like an ancient, primitive hunter, he would have one chance. Failure meant death. He was a silent, unseen figure. The man astride the horse, one hand on the butt of his gun in its holster, peered across the lake. It was his horse that sensed Fargo moving closer. The animal moved, blew air through its nostrils. "Whoa, dammit," the man hissed. They were his last words. Fargo, almost at the horse's side, propelled himself upward, clasped one hand over the man's mouth while with his other hand he yanked the man's head in a half-circle. He felt the crack of vertebrae, and the figure went limp, toppling from the saddle into his arms.

The horse bolted, the instant of silence shattered. Fargo heard the nearest rider wheel his horse and shout. On one knee, Fargo yanked the man's gun from its holster. The horseman was racing down at him, another following a dozen yards behind. Fargo took aim, and fired. . . .

BE SURE TO READ THE OTHER THRILLING NOVELS IN THE EXCITING *TRAILSMAN* SERIES!

THE
TRAILSMAN
#193

BULLETS
AND
BRIDLES

by

Jon Sharpe

A SIGNET BOOK

SIGNET
Published by the Penguin Group
Penguin Putnam Inc., 375 Hudson Street,
New York, New York 10014, U.S.A.
Penguin Books Ltd, 27 Wrights Lane,
London W8 5TZ, England
Penguin Books Australia Ltd,
Ringwood, Victoria, Australia
Penguin Books Canada Ltd, 10 Alcorn Avenue,
Toronto, Ontario, Canada M4V 3B2
Penguin Books (N.Z.) Ltd, 182–190 Wairau Road,
Auckland 10, New Zealand

Penguin Books Ltd, Registered Offices:
Harmondsworth, Middlesex, England

First published by Signet, an imprint of Dutton Signet,
a member of Penguin Putnam Inc.

First Printing, January, 1998
10 9 8 7 6 5 4 3 2 1

The first chapter of this book originally appeared in *Durango Duel*,
the one hundred ninety-second volume in this series.

Ⓓ REGISTERED TRADEMARK—MARCA REGISTRADA

Printed in the United States of America

The Trailsman

Beginnings . . . they bend the tree and they mark the man. Skye Fargo was born when he was eighteen. Terror was his midwife, vengeance his first cry. Killing spawned Skye Fargo, ruthless, cold-blooded murder. Out of the acrid smoke of gunpowder still hanging in the air, he rose, cried out a promise never forgotten.

The Trailsman they began to call him all across the West: searcher, scout, hunter, the man who could see where others only looked, his skills for hire but not his soul, the man who lived each day to the fullest, yet trailed each tomorrow. Skye Fargo, the Trailsman, and the seeker who could take the wildness of a land and the wanting of a woman and make them his own.

*Kansas, 1860, west of Pawnee Rock,
a land where pounding hooves and
pounding passions turned greed
into hate and hate into killing . . .*

1

"Trouble."

The big man with the lake blue eyes spat the word softly as he listened to the night. Listening was part of him, listening, sensing, feeling. The night was heavy, with that ominous stillness that all too often spelled trouble of one kind or another. He had become a believer in harbingers, portents that chose their own time and their own way to send their veiled messages. His lips pulled back in a grimace as he leaned back against the red cedar and stared out into the stillness. Not even the soft scurrying of field mice or the chatter of fox broke the silence. With another soft curse, he shook away thoughts of harbingers and let his mind turn to anticipation.

It was, after all, anticipation that had brought him to the rich Kansas plains. Anticipation had a name, Carol Harwood, a face of green-flecked, hazel eyes and sandy hair and a body of long, lithe electricity. The memories flooded over him again, Carol's long body entwined around his, her breasts pressed into his mouth, deep the way she liked. It had been that way between them from the very beginning, from the first time he'd broken trail for her pa, Ed Harwood. Carol had wanted him at once, and as he found out,

Carol usually had her way. They had been wonderful times, ending only when her pa unexpectedly died. Carol decided to take her sizable inheritance and move from Iowa. She'd wanted him to go with her. "I've been planning," she'd said. "There's big money to be made in horses."

"I'm no wrangler," he'd told her and they had quarreled, Carol bitter, demanding, using all her passion to convince him. But he had gone his way finally, yet Carol had stayed in touch, her letters arriving with the regularity of the seasons, asking, inviting, reminding him of fervid nights. Sometimes he wondered if she still really wanted him that much or she couldn't stand not getting her way. And now opportunity, work, and time had combined to bring him close enough to visit and he was still surprised at how strongly anticipation had taken hold. Good enough reason to turn away portents and harbingers, he told himself.

Skye Fargo finished his meal of cold antelope jerky, undressed to his underwear, and stretched out atop his bedroll in the warm Kansas night. He closed his eyes and let sleep finally wrap itself around him as the night stayed heavy and still. But he slept uneasily, though he'd no idea how many hours had gone by when he snapped awake, instantly aware of the faint swooshing sound. Whitetails leaping through the air, he knew at once as he sat up and caught sight of a half a dozen of the deer sailing by as though they were propelled by invisible springs. They were in the kind of long, sweeping bounds that meant they sensed a danger only headlong flight could answer. As they disappeared into the night, he saw the orange glow lighting the sky, distant yet not distant enough for the deer.

Fargo pulled on clothes as he saw the glow grow brighter and he leaped onto the Ovaro without pausing to saddle up. He headed for the orange glow, watched it grow deeper, redder, and he squinted hard. No prairie fire, he decided with a measure of relief. Prairie fires were quick to spread horizontally. These flames stayed in place and fed on something contained, and he swore as he urged the Ovaro faster. When he crossed a low rise the flames became clear, reaching skyward, and he saw the burning timbers of the house they consumed with almost gleeful abandon. The screams of horses came to him as he closed in and he saw the double row of long barns behind the house. Flames were licking at their edges as they leaped from the burning house, the horses screaming in panic.

Fargo reined to a halt and leaped to the ground, his glance taking in the long, fenced corrals that stretched from the barns. He was running, on his way to the barns, when he glimpsed the shape through the smoke and flame, a figure lying but a few feet from the leaping flames on what was once the porch of the house. He changed direction and ran toward the figure as he ducked away from a falling timber that toppled from the house. Reaching the figure, he leaned down and saw a young woman clothed in a gray nightgown. She was alive, the soft touch of her breath brushing his face. As he gathered the unconscious woman in his arms, he twisted away from another length of falling beam.

He put her down on the ground when he was far enough from the burning house to be beyond falling scattering bits of wood and ember. He paused for a moment, saw that her breathing was steady, and noted the bruise at the top of her temple. She'd come around in time, he was satisfied, and he left her to race toward the barns, where smoke now sifted into both rows. Spying the corral gates, he paused to open four of them before he ran to the side doors of the first barn. Pulling the doors open, he went inside and began kicking and pulling open stall gates, leaping back at once as the horses thundered past him out of the stalls and out of the barn. He did the same at the second row of barns, somehow managing not to be trampled. The fleeing horses did exactly what he'd hoped they would. Instead of running back into the barns as panic-stricken horses often did, they fled through the opened corral gates.

Fargo stepped away from the barn, aware that there was absolutely nothing he could do single-handedly to stop the fire that had begun to consume both barns. He started to go through the nearest corral gate when the shots exploded, one splintering the top of the corral gate inches from his head. He threw himself flat on the ground in a headlong dive as another three shots grazed him. Rolling, he came up against the side of the corral as he yanked the Colt from its holster and saw three men running toward him. Three more came up from the right side, he saw. He fired and two of the figures went down, falling into each other as the others scattered. But Fargo was on his feet and running, all too aware that silhouetted by the flames behind him, he was a perfect target.

He saw a water trough and catapulted himself through the air, landing behind it as more shots rang out, four of them thudding into the trough. He lay flat, crawled forward, and peered around one end of the long trough. The figures had spread out as they advanced toward him. He took aim and fired, and one of the figures spun as he fell. The others halted and started to back away, laying down a barrage of shots to cover their retreat. Fargo stayed down until the shots ended. He poked his head up and saw three figures reach their horses, which were standing against a thin line of red cedar. But they weren't about to flee, he was certain. They just wanted greater mobility in coming after him again. He pushed to his feet and raced to where he had left the Ovaro; the young woman still lay unconscious on the ground. He leaped onto the Ovaro as the three horsemen came toward him. When he saw a small stand of black oak, he sent the pinto into it. He let the horse crash noisily through the oak and saw the three riders veer to charge after him. When they were into the trees, he swung one leg over the Ovaro's pure white back and slid from the horse.

The Ovaro went on and Fargo dropped to one knee. He had the Colt raised as the riders charged after the Ovaro. He took the first down with one shot, then the second man, who tried to veer away and found he was too late. Fargo whirled as the third horseman didn't follow. The third man started charging at him from behind. Fargo fired and realized his shot was too high as the horse hurtled into him. Diving sideways, Fargo felt the front legs of the horse slam into his side, flinging him upward and into a tree trunk. He gasped in pain as he fell to the ground and knew he was lucky the horse's chest hadn't bowled into him. He lay down and shook his head and tried to clear away the yellow and red lights that flashed inside his head.

Fighting away pain, he shook his head again and the lights stopped exploding inside him. He heard the sound of footsteps crashing through the brush and pushed himself away from the tree and managed to half turn in time to see the figure rushing at him. Fargo tried to bring his hand up but the man's blow swept it aside and Fargo felt himself knocked backward. He fell against the tree trunk, realizing the Colt was no longer in his hand. The figure in front of him grew clear for an instant and Fargo saw the man aiming a hard right at him. As he jerked his head sideways, he could feel the blow whistling past him and could hear the man cursing in pain as his fist slammed into the tree. Summoning up strength out of desperation, Fargo drove himself upward as he kept his head down. He felt the sharp pain as his head slammed into the man's jaw, sending the man backward and down. Fargo brought his head up. The man was on his back, the gun still in his hand.

Fargo brought his foot down onto the man's belly and the man cried out as his legs came up, his shot going wildly into the trees. Fargo bent down and pulled him around as he brought his arm up to fire. Fargo's pile-driver blow came down on the man, crashing into his arm, driving it into his body just as he fired again. Fargo winced as the bullet blew the man's jaw off and the figure went limp. Stepping back, Fargo cursed softly, drew in a deep breath, and searched on the ground until he found his Colt. Holstering the gun, he rummaged through the man's pockets and found nothing to identify him. He straightened up and didn't bother to search the other two he passed as he walked to where the Ovaro had stopped.

They wouldn't have anything to identify them, either, he knew. But a new and terrible realization swept through him as he walked the Ovaro out of the trees. He hadn't come upon a fire caused by carelessness or accident. No cigarette left burning, no lamp overturned, no candle catching a curtain had set this fire. It had been deliberately set to consume everything, the house and anyone in it, the barns and all the horses. They had plainly just finished their ruthless task when he'd reached the fire. They had seen him get the horses out and come back to get him, no doubt infuriated that he'd foiled at least part of their plan. The terrible enormity of it continued to grow inside him as he emerged from the trees and stared at the scene. The barns were burning down and only blackened, charred timbers remained of the house, smoke spiraling upward in a dozen separate whorls.

As he walked closer he saw the young woman where he had left her, but she was sitting up. She turned to him as he came up. "You've come around," he said and saw deep brown eyes round with dazed shock. He caught a hint of fear come into her eyes. "You were unconscious when I found you on the porch," he said. In the glow of the still-burning barns, he saw short, brown hair, a face with even features under the smudges of ash, a well-shaped mouth, even hanging open as it was. The shapeless gray nightgown hid the rest of her.

"You found me," she repeated, shock still slowing her reactions.

"Yes," he said. "I saw the flames and came by."

She swallowed, pulled her mouth closed, and he saw nice, full lips. A frown crossed her smudged, bruised forehead as thoughts fought their way through the shock still clinging to her. "Andy. Did you see Andy?" she asked, fear coming into her voice.

"Who's Andy?" Fargo asked.

"My best friend. My ranch foreman," she said. "His room's in the rear of the house."

"There's no house left," Fargo said gently.

The deep brown eyes blinked back at him. "Find Andy. You've got to find Andy. Oh God, please," she half whispered. He nodded and went past her along the edge of the smoking remains of the house, his lips drawn in a tight line. If Andy had been inside the house, he'd certainly have been burned to death, probably beyond recognition. Fargo peered through the wispy spirals of smoke and scanned the charred timbers that had once been a house. He saw nothing that resembled a body and doubted he'd have recognized one if he saw it. He turned to go back when he spotted the shape on the ground a dozen yards away. He hurried to the figure and saw a man clothed in a red flannel nightshirt, short gray hair atop a face that held at least sixty years in it. He leaned down and saw that the man was dead.

But not from the fire, Fargo grunted as he saw the three bullet holes in the red flannel nightshirt, each surrounded by a stain of darker red. The man had been fleeing the house when he was gunned down. Fargo cursed softly, rose, and walked back to where the young woman waited. She hadn't moved and there was still shock in her face as she looked up. "You find him?" she asked, the note of fearful hope in her voice cutting into him.

"He wear a red flannel nightshirt?" Fargo asked softly.

"Always," she nodded.

"I found him," Fargo said, and she stared up at him as the unsaid slowly sank into her.

"Oh God. Oh my God," she said, her hands going to her face. He waited and let her fight back tears until she finally brought her eyes back to him. "The horses?" she asked, her voice hardly a whisper.

"I got them out, all of them," Fargo said.

"Thank God. Oh, thank God," she murmured.

"I let them go out of the corral so they wouldn't run back inside in panic. They're all over the countryside by now," he said.

"We'll round them up," the young woman said.

"We?" Fargo questioned.

"My hands. They'll be coming back sometime tonight. Tomorrow they'll go out and round up the horses," she said and started to push herself up. He offered a helping hand and saw that standing, she was no more than medium height, although she looked shorter in the shapeless nightgown. Her deep brown eyes searched his face. "I owe you, real big. Who are you, mister?" she asked.

"Name's Fargo . . . Skye Fargo."

A tiny furrow creased her smudged brow. "I've heard that name. You the one they call the Trailsman?"

"Sometimes," he conceded.

"I'm Darcy Ingram," she said, holding out a small but firm, smooth hand. "This terrible night was no accident," she said gravely.

"I know," he said quietly and saw the surprise slide across her even features.

"They tried to kill me, too," Fargo said. "They wanted to stop me from letting the horses out."

"The bastards," Darcy Ingram spit out.

"They give you that bruise on your forehead?" he asked.

"Yes, but I didn't see anyone. When the fire started, I woke and ran outside. I never made it off the porch. Someone was waiting and hit me," Darcy said.

"And left you on the porch for the fire to finish off," Fargo said.

"Everybody knows I give my hands Thursday night off. They just waited till only Andy and I were here," Darcy said.

"Why?" Fargo questioned.

"Because there are a lot of rotten, no-good bastards around here," she snapped. "It'll take too long to tell you, now. Let's talk tomorrow. Can you come back? I'd like you to."

"Guess so," Fargo said.

"I'll expect you. Now, I'll wait here till my hands come back later tonight," she said.

"What then? You're all burned out?" Fargo asked.

"See those hawthorns over there?" she said, gesturing to a small cluster of trees. "I've a cabin just behind them, use it for guests, mostly. I'll stay there till we've time to rebuild. The bunkhouse hasn't been touched, so the hands will have their place," she said, and he found the long bunkhouse beyond the corrals. "I've a few things to wear at the cabin and I'll buy new things in town, later." Her hand reached out, pressed his arm. "I can't tell you how grateful I am to you, Fargo, but that's not the only reason I want you to come back."

"It might not be for a day or so. I'll be going to Foxville, first, then I'll be paying a visit," Fargo told her.

"Foxville's the only town near here," Darcy said. "You can't miss it."

"Good enough. I'll stop back soon as I can," Fargo said.

"Whatever's best for you. I'll still be busy rounding up horses. There are some sixty of them to bring in," she said.

"There's something else to clean up," Fargo said. "Six of them, three near the corrals, three in the black oak."

Her mouth tightened. "I'll see to it. I know just how I'll do it," Darcy said, her voice ice. He peered at her but her face stayed an expressionless mask. She went with him as he walked to the Ovaro and her eyes took in the magnificent jet black fore-and-hindquarters and pure white midsection of the horse. "That's a fine horse," she said admiringly.

"It is," he said and her hands came up, pressed against his chest.

"Promise you'll come back, Fargo," Darcy said.

"Promise," he nodded. She lifted herself onto her toes, a quick, impulsive gesture and her lips brushed his cheek.

"Thanks again, for everything. I'm not good with words," she said.

"That'll do," he said. Up close, her small nose had an upturned pugnaciousness to it, he saw. Darcy was plainly an independent young woman and he pushed aside the questions about her that went through his mind. They'd have to wait for his next visit. He pulled himself onto the pinto and waved at her as he sent the horse into a trot. The acrid smell of burnt wood and drifting smoke stayed with him as he rode back to where he had left his bedroll. The orange glow no longer lit the distant darkness as he reined to a halt, slid from the horse, and pulled off his clothes.

He stretched out on the bedroll and the night remained still and ominous, he noted. But then, harbingers and portents never just vanished. They had a way of clinging, staying on to remind one that they were never an end but only a beginning.

2

When he woke, the sun had chased away the night and with it all the ominous stillness. Harbingers, like criminals and vampires, flee from brightness. Fargo used his canteen to wash, found a stand of wild plums for breakfast, and unhurriedly made his way east. But the scent of burned wood came to his nostrils as he drew closer to Darcy Ingram's place and he turned to skirt the area. Riding on, he found a narrow road bordered by the softness of red ash, with their light green leaves and velvety twigs, that eventually led him past wide plains and into Foxville by the late morning. "Ask Sheriff Bailey in town," Carol had written in one note. "He'll give you directions to my place." Foxville itself was larger, more crowded, and more prosperous a town than he had expected, Fargo noted as he rode slowly down the main street.

He saw a proper bank with a curtained window, a small church, and a white-painted town meeting hall, along with the usual saloon and small stores. A number of one-horse farm wagons moved along the street, some with extension couplers, along with heavier, high-sided seed-bed wagons. He saw plenty of buckboards and even a ladies' driving phaeton.

When he found the sheriff's office, marked by a sign in the window of a narrow-frame, wood structure, he also saw a small cluster of men gathered outside. He reined to a halt, dismounted, and started to move through the men when their words came to him and he slowed.

"They found old Andy Pettigrew shot dead," Fargo heard someone say and he halted to listen further.

"Burned down her whole place," someone else said. "One of her hands was at the general store buying blankets this morning." A man stepped from the building, a star-shaped badge pinned to a dark blue shirt, and Fargo took in a square face with dark eyebrows and pepper-and-salt hair, a man of medium height, broad-chested and authoritative in his brusque stride. He wore a Remington in his holster, a six-shot, single-action army issue, Fargo noted.

"Any more news, Sheriff?" one of the men asked.

"Nothin' more to tell," the sheriff said brusquely.

"We heard Darcy Ingram had her boys bring in six bodies," someone called out.

"That's right," the sheriff said.

"Had them dumped on the doorstep of the Wranglers' Association," another man put in. "Why?"

"You'll have to ask her that," the sheriff said, irritation rising in his voice. "Darcy Ingram's got a strange sense of humor."

"Seems like she was saying something," the questioner said. Fargo agreed silently, though the act did carry a certain macabre humor in it which made him smile inwardly.

"It was probably her way of saying I don't give her

enough protection. She's always complained about that," the sheriff growled.

"We heard somebody came by, saved her neck and her horses from the fire," someone else said. Fargo considered a moment more and decided to speak out.

"You heard right," he said and everyone turned to him. "I happened to be near," he added.

The sheriff frowned at him. "Well, now, who might you be, mister?" he asked.

"Fargo . . . Skye Fargo."

"Were you there when the fire broke out?" the sheriff queried.

"Not when it started. I was bedded down on the plains. The flames woke me up and when I rode to see what it was, I found her place already mostly burned up," Fargo said.

"Step inside, Fargo," the sheriff said, and Fargo followed the man into a small office with a battered wooden desk and three jail cells taking up the rest of the space. "You know anything about the six men Darcy had dumped here in town?" the sheriff asked.

"They set the fire. They tried to kill me, too," Fargo said.

The sheriff peered at him. "You saying you . . ." he began and Fargo cut him off.

"I'm saying I didn't much favor that idea," Fargo answered.

The sheriff's stare deepened. "I can understand that," he said slowly. "You must be somethin' special with a six-gun."

"Sometimes," Fargo said laconically.

"Seems to me you not only saved Darcy Ingram's neck but did in a passel of rustlers," the sheriff said.

"Rustlers?" Fargo frowned.

"That's right. We get a lot of them around here," the man said.

"Rustlers want to steal horses, not set them on fire," Fargo said.

"They set the fire so's the horses would break out and they'd be waiting to drive them off," the sheriff said.

"The men who came at me were on foot at first. They weren't waiting to drive off any horses," Fargo answered.

"There were probably more of them you didn't see," the sheriff said, and Fargo felt the irritation rise inside him. The man didn't want to listen to logic. He was content with his own explanation. Why, Fargo wondered. Perhaps the sheriff preferred his explanation because it was the easiest one. Or was there something else? But the men hadn't been rustlers, Fargo was certain. "What brings you to Foxville, Fargo?" the sheriff asked, breaking into his thoughts.

"Came looking for you. You are Sheriff Bailey, right?" Fargo said.

"I am," the man said, his brows lifting.

"Carol Harwood wrote that you could give me directions to her place," Fargo said.

"Yes, but I can do better. She's at the Wranglers' Association meeting. I'll take you there. It's just a short walk," Bailey said. Fargo followed the man into the street as the Ovaro tagged along behind. The sheriff halted a hundred yards on before a low-roofed, unpainted wooden building, the door hanging open. The voices came clearly from inside the building.

"She's still around. That's the only thing I'm sorry about," one of the voices said.

"We all feel that way but you don't want to go around saying it," another voice said.

"Why not? It's no secret how she feels about us," the first voice said.

"Excuse me, folks," the sheriff said, hurrying forward into the building, and Fargo followed on his heels into a large room with a long table and chairs. Four men clustered together, all well dressed and to one side he saw Carol, her tall, lithe body clothed in a white, tailored shirt and a dark green skirt. She turned as he entered, the green-flecked, hazel eyes widening in astonishment, her sandy hair shorter than it used to be.

"Surprise," Fargo said softly.

"My God," she gasped and was across the room instantly, her arms around him. "I don't believe it. Good God, you're finally here," she said.

"Got the chance," he said as she clung to him.

"God, what a wonderful, wonderful surprise," Carol said. "We have so much to talk about." Her arm linked in his, she turned to the men looking on. "This is an old and very special friend, Skye Fargo, the Trailsman," she introduced.

"Good to meet you, Fargo," a heavyset, beefy-faced man said, his hair very black, a heavy, brooding quality to him. "Any friend of Carol's is a friend of ours. Ed Buckley here."

Fargo nodded at the man as Carol turned to another man. "Amos Stockel," she said.

"Welcome, Fargo, welcome," the man beamed, his voice loud, his manner effusive. But his eyes were a cold blue and Fargo wondered if the heartiness was a mask.

Carol turned to the third figure, a man with a self-indulgent face with pale blue eyes and brown hair, of medium height with the beginnings of a paunch showing under an expensive gray frock coat with a diamond stickpin. "Dave Cord," she said.

"What brings you to Foxville, Fargo?" the man asked, trying to sound merely curious and failing. Fargo recognized the voice as the one that had made the sour comments about Darcy Ingram.

"Social call on Carol," Fargo said. The fourth man was tall with an angular figure and a lean, drawn face with deep-set eyes. The smile didn't change the severeness in his face, Fargo noted.

"Marty Schotter," Carol said. Fargo took the outstretched hand and found a strong grip.

"This is the feller who saved Darcy Ingram's neck," Sheriff Bailey cut in and Fargo saw Carol's eyes widen as they looked at him.

"Really?" she murmured.

"Saw the flames and went to help," Fargo said.

"That was a wonderful thing to do," Carol said and turned to the others. "But that's the kind of thing I'd expect from Fargo," she said.

Fargo held a wry smile as his eyes swept the four men. "I get the feeling you're not unhappy about what happened to Darcy Ingram," he said.

"We're not friendly with her, that's for sure," Dave Cord said.

"But, of course, nobody here wants to see her hurt," Amos Stockel added hastily. "Sheriff says it was rustlers."

"You all agree?" Fargo inquired mildly.

"I'd go along with whatever Sheriff Bailey says," Ed Buckley answered, and the others murmured agreement. "Though she's made some real enemies. Ask Sid Bundy about her," the man added.

"Enough talk about Darcy Ingram," Carol interrupted, keeping her arm linked in Fargo's. "We're finished here. I'm taking Fargo with me."

"Nice to meet everybody," Fargo said as Carol pulled him to the door and the others offered pleasant good-byes. Outside, Carol halted before a green-painted buckboard.

"Hitch your horse to the back and ride with me," she said. Fargo hitched the Ovaro behind the wagon. He slid in beside Carol and she drove quickly from town. When they were on a dirt road, she pulled the horse to a halt and turned to him. Her lips were pressed hard on his at once, her kiss long, moist, made of memories and promises. When she pulled back, his hand traced an invisible line along the length of her jaw, the straight nose, the coolly patrician features, both delicate and strong at the same time. He half smiled at the thin eyebrows that seemed always slightly arched in an expression of constant skepticism. "I gave up expecting you'd ever come," Carol murmured.

"Never give up expecting," he said as she took up the reins again. "Seems you've done exactly what you said you were going to do, made money with horses. And done well at it." She allowed a small smile of agreement. "This Wranglers' Association, you part of it or just friends with them?"

"Part of it." she said, turning north at a pyramid-shaped rock, and driving across flatland dotted with red ash. "We round up, break, and sell our own horses to our own customers but we cooperate with each other. For example, we usually drive our herds together."

"You keep them all straight at the end of the drive?" Fargo questioned.

"They're all branded by then, so there's no problem in sorting them out. My brand's the double *C*, Dave Cord's a barbed *D*, Amos Stockel has a lazy *S*, Marty Schotter a triple rail, Ed Buckley a long *B*. There's no confusion. As I said, we work together."

"Except for Darcy Ingram," Fargo remarked.

"That's right," Carol said with ice in her voice.

"Who do you sell to?" Fargo asked.

"Mostly eastern and southern buyers. They want sturdy riding horses, workhorses, some jumpers and show stock. We sell a few horses to the army, but they have their own sources. Mostly, we sell mustangs and quarter horses with a few pintos."

"Why isn't Darcy Ingram in your association?" Fargo asked.

"She wouldn't join. She's stubborn, thinks she's better than anybody else. She's full of crazy ideas of her own. That's why nobody's really sorry about what happened to her. Maybe she'll go her way, now," Carol said. Fargo made no comment, though he had the feeling that Darcy Ingram didn't plan to go away. The houses came into sight, a long, low main house, bunkhouses, stables, and barns spread out from it with large white-painted corral fences flanking the buildings. Carol drew up to the front door of the main house and Fargo took in a solid structure fashioned of heavy timbers with a shingled roof. Swinging from the buckboard, Fargo unhitched the pinto. "Go inside. I'll be right back after I put the rig away," Carol said and drove to a large shed.

A half-dozen hands waved to her as she drove by, and then went back to working with some dozen horses in the nearest corral. Fargo went into the house and found himself in a large living room well furnished with a leather sofa, a large secretary desk of glistening cherry, heavy chairs, and floors covered with quilted rugs. "Looks as though you're doing real well for yourself," Fargo said to Carol when she returned.

"I am and I aim to do better," Carol said, drawing him down on the sofa. "We'll be making our fall drive for the eastern buyers in a few days. Maybe you can be part of it."

"Maybe," he allowed, and she leaned forward, arms encircling his neck.

"Seeing you is making yesterday explode inside me. I never imagined it would be this overwhelming," she said. "But it is and I'm not going to play coy."

"You never were one for that," Fargo remembered aloud and felt her mouth close on his. She rose and pulled him with her into a large bedroom of soft powder blue sheets, pillows, and matching curtains. He felt the wanting surge through him as she began to unbutton his shirt, her unvarnished hunger reaching out. Clothes fell from her as he undressed and he heard his own swift intake of breath as she stood naked before him, beauty making a mockery of memory. He drank in the longish breasts that hung with graceful beauty, swaying ever so slightly as she moved, each tipped with a tiny nipple of the palest pink, smaller than he remembered them. Her narrow-waisted, long, lean body glided, flat stomach almost concave and just below, the small triangle with an adolescent neatness to it.

Her legs just missing being thin, thighs and calves carrying enough flesh for long, lovely curves, her skin a soft white, almost milky, almost exactly as he remembered. Carol pulled him onto the powder blue sheets, her breasts against his face instantly, seeking, pushing. He parted his lips and felt the tiny, pale pink nipple brush over his face, a sweet softness in it, move against him, push into his mouth and he heard the pages turning back to yesterday. "Oh, oh God." Carol breathed, pushing deeper and rotating her breast gently inside his mouth as she gasped and shuddered in pleasure. "Yes, yes . . . just the way it was, just the same," she murmured. He let his tongue circle the edges of the small areola, felt the wispy, threadlike little hairs, pulling gently as Carol gave a soft, soughing sound.

She pressed deeper into his mouth with a sudden savagery he also remembered and she seemed to explode, her hands becoming little fists that struck against his chest and shoulders. Her legs lifted, clamping around him, her body almost slamming into him. Groaning, she rubbed herself against his firm, muscled torso, rubbing the small, rounded bulge of her Venus mound up and down over his groin, letting him feel the tactile excitement of her neat little triangle. "You remember, you remember, just as I do," she breathed.

"Couldn't be forgetting," he said honestly. Carol moved as he pressed his pulsating maleness into the soft-wire tendrils. She twisted her torso, pressing herself harder against him, the long, lithe legs tightening. His hand moved slowly and languorously along her body, caressing the softness of her convex little belly and moving along the inside of one thigh. Her legs fell open for him. He touched the bottom of her thigh and felt the spreading dampness of her as he reached the dark, warm portal.

"Yes, yes . . . oh, yes, please, please," Carol murmured and kept his mouth clasped to her breast as her hips lifted, offering, the entreaty of the flesh, the invitation beyond refusing. He moved further and touched the smooth, wet, and waiting lips. Carol's cry was made of pure pleasure, the song of eros given voice that became a long, low, moaning sound. He slid along the lubricous walls and felt their quivering smoothness, the touch of touches, and paused to drink in the tactile beauty that surrounded him, pressed against him, responding as it gave, the total, complete exchange of the senses. "Yes, yes, the way it was . . . oh, God, the way it was," Carol breathed and he felt her trembling grow stronger until her entire body shook and her long, low moans grew stronger. Her hands tightened against him and her moans became short, almost urgent little gasps, each louder than the one before.

He waited for the sharp, fierce, piercing cry, the signal it had always been and plunged forward inside her and Carol's legs slapped against him and her hips twisted from side to side as though she were possessed by feelings beyond possessing. "Oh, yes, yes, yes," she screamed and every memoried sensation came alive again. Her frenzied passion swept him along and he cried out with her, became one with her every twisting, pumping motion. When her long body stiffened, seeming to hang in midair, the final, culminating scream tore from her and he exploded with her, the senses demanding nothing less than total surrender. It had always been that way with Carol and it was that way once again, the absolute fierceness of her passion overwhelming, consuming. He lay beside her, listening to the long, harsh sounds of her deep breaths until she finally calmed and pushed herself up on one elbow, one longish breast swaying beautifully. "You've got to stay, Fargo. You can't go off again," Carol said.

"No promises," he said gently.

She gave a wry smile. "I remember that," she said. "I've more to offer, now."

"You know that won't mean anything," he said and her lovely, bare shoulders lifted in a shrug.

"We'll see," she said, a touch of smugness in her voice. "I have to meet with some southern buyers. We're meeting at Eden Flats alongside the Cimarron in Oklahoma Territory. If I'd known you were coming I'd have changed it but I can't, now."

"Wouldn't expect you to," he said.

"I'll be back in a day, maybe two at most. I want you to use my place till I get back, just stay here and relax. Then we'll have time to really turn back the clock. This was only a beginning," Carol said.

"Pretty good beginning," he said as he admired her long, lithe beauty.

"Please stay here. I like the idea of hurrying back, knowing you'll be waiting here," Carol said.

"You've a deal," he said, the thought of relaxing in the comfort of a soft bed and luxurious surroundings too good to turn down. Besides, he had no reason to refuse the offer.

"I've a woman who cooks for me. She'll have a good jackrabbit stew ready by now," Carol said, rising and putting on a robe of dark blue. He swung from the bed, pulled on his clothes, and followed her to a formal dining room where the woman had the table set. "This is Maria," Carol said and Fargo nodded at a short, somewhat squat woman of middle age, a face bearing the heavy features of mixed Apache blood. But her cooking was light and delicious, the meal a pleasure-filled interlude, and when it was over, Carol led him back to her bedroom. "Maria will make breakfast for you in the morning," she said, shedding the robe and stretching out on the bed. "And I'll make love to you come night."

"Sounds too good to be true," he said, pulling off his clothes. Carol quickly proved it was very much true as she filled the night with her cries of pleasure. Later, he slept wrapped in her arms, her long body draped around him, every part of her deliciously sensual, awake or asleep. When morning came, he woke to find her dressed in jeans and a tailored shirt, looking beautifully crisp.

"Don't get up," she said. "Tomorrow night, if I can get back in time, the night after for sure. It's time you waited. Goodness knows I've done enough of it."

"Fair enough." He laughed and she hurried from the room, her long body swaying with a softness that contrasted with the purposefulness of her stride. He lay back, relaxed a little while longer, and finally rose, washed, and dressed. He found the housekeeper had left coffee and sweet rolls waiting in the dining room and after breakfasting, he strolled outside. He watched the hands working the horses in two corrals when a tall, thinly built man came toward him. He had a pleasant face with unruly, dark brown hair and offered a quick smile.

33

"Jeff Cotter. I'm Miss Carol's foreman," he said. "You're Fargo. She told me to watch for you. Your horse is in stable one."

"Much obliged," Fargo said as the man walked beside him toward the stable.

"You worked long for Carol?" Fargo queried casually.

"About a year," Jeff Cotter said. "She pays good wages but nobody slacks off on her."

"Fair's fair."

"I've no complaints," the ranch foreman said.

"You know much about the others in the Wranglers' Association?"

"Not a lot." Jeff Cotter said.

"What about Darcy Ingram?" Fargo asked.

"Met her in town from time to time. She's a spitfire but I never had any trouble with her. She pretty much minds her own business and so do I," Cotter said, but there was no reproach in his voice. They reached the stable and Fargo found the Ovaro in a large corner stall. "He's been fed," Jeff Cotter said as Fargo saddled the horse.

"Thanks," Fargo said, tightening the cinch and pulling himself into the saddle. "You know a man named Sid Bundy?" he asked.

"I know he's a real unfriendly man, hardly ever comes into town except after dark, lives by himself and wants it that way," Jeff Cotter said. "He doesn't take to anybody anytime."

"Where's his place?" Fargo inquired.

"Due north. Go past the pyramid rock, turn right, and ride into the low hills. A wide river runs through his land. You'll see it just back of his house."

"I heard he's got a real dislike of Darcy Ingram," Fargo mentioned.

"So I've heard. Whatever happened between them was before my time around here," Cotter said.

"Much obliged," Fargo said, and Cotter waved back as he put the Ovaro into a slow trot. There was nothing to be gained by questioning Jeff Cotter further, Fargo realized. The man wasn't holding back. He was smart enough to keep his distance, not ask too much, learn too much, involve himself too much. But the question that stayed lodged in Fargo's mind wouldn't go away. He'd never been one for unfinished, unexplained things. They nagged at him, made him feel as though he were carrying a burden he had to shed. Rustlers hadn't set fire to Darcy Ingram's place and he wondered why most everyone seemed so quick to accept that, Carol included.

Perhaps that was only natural on her part, given the dislike she had for Darcy Ingram. Maybe that could apply to the other members of the Wranglers' Association. Yet it bothered him, just as Sheriff Bailey's eagerness to push that explanation bothered him. They were all quick to cry rustlers but perhaps not for the same reasons. Was their dislike of Darcy Ingram just the dislike of a thorny competitor? That was the picture Carol had painted, but he wondered if there was more, perhaps more than Carol was willing to admit. Or more than she actually realized herself.

He had only spent a few minutes with her friends in the association but he didn't need more than that. He was the Trailsman. He knew how to read signs, in faces as well as forests, and these men were a hard-bitten, callous lot, men who valued money and possessions before anything else. It was in the turn of their mouths and the coldness of their eyes. How well did Carol know them, Fargo asked himself. But the one question continued to ride with him and he didn't have to worry about that. The men who'd set Darcy Ingram's place on fire, willing to destroy all her horses, weren't out to rustle anything. He turned the pinto west, rode leisurely, and the acrid odor of burnt wood still hung in the air as he neared what had been Darcy Ingram's place.

The still-smoldering remains came into sight, looking not unlike charred skeletons of what had been a house, stables, barns. The corrals were still intact and in surprise he saw some twenty horses inside one, guarded by a single cowhand. Darcy Ingram stepped from the line of hawthorns and he reined to a halt and dismounted. He had a proper look at her for the first time. The shapeless nightdress was gone, in its place, dusty jeans, a yellow shirt, and a yellow ribbon in the short brown hair. He took in a young woman not nearly as tall as Carol, with a compact, tight figure and brisk, determined steps. The yellow shirt rested on what seemed modest but high breasts and the jeans were filled with rounded hips and solid legs. No longer smoke-smudged, her face held a saucy, pert prettiness with a small, upturned nose, deep brown eyes, soft cheeks, eyes set wide apart, and a mouth of full, almost thick lips. It was a face that avoided ordinariness by the pleasant open prettiness in it.

"I see you've got yourself some stock back already. I'm surprised," Fargo said.

"The boys have been out rounding up horses since dawn. Most of them were still out. Thanks to you, there are horses to round up," Darcy Ingram said and her hand reached out, pressed into his arm as her dark brown eyes peered at him. "I'll never be able to thank you enough, or the angel that brought you here at the right time," she said.

"What happened is the talk of the town," he said. "Your visit, too," he added blandly.

"Good." She snorted.

"Showing there are all kinds of ways to make a statement," he said and smiled.

"Why not?" she returned.

"You have anyone in the Wranglers' Association particularly in mind?" he asked mildly.

"Any and all," she said, her upturned nose turning up further.

"I came to Foxville to visit one of them. Carol Harwood," Fargo said.

Darcy's eyes flashed at once. "Forget what I said about an angel bringing you here," she said. "You come to see her looking for work?"

"No. I knew her and her folks back in Iowa, decided to come visit after all this time," Fargo explained and saw the instant anger slide from Darcy's face. "Besides, that's not important. I was near, that's what mattered."

"I guess so," she agreed. "And I'm real grateful for that." She took his arm and he felt the firm compactness of her against him. "I've coffee on in the cabin. Let's talk there," she said and led the way through a small pathway that opened in the hawthorns. The cabin appeared, larger than the usual cabin, solidly built with two large rooms inside, a fireplace, and a small wood-burning Franklin stove. His eyes moved over the interior as Darcy Ingram poured coffee from a white enamel kettle. "Andy built most of it," she said. She paused, her eyes filling at once. With a pugnacious tilt of her chin, she fought back tears. "The bastards," she hissed, letting anger come to her aid.

"Some folks say it was rustlers," Fargo remarked.

"I expect some folks would," Darcy shot back.

"Sheriff Bailey was one of them," Fargo mentioned.

"Didn't you see his strings?" Darcy said and Fargo let one eyebrow rise. "He's a damn puppet," she said.

"I hear there are other folks who aren't real fond of you," Fargo remarked.

"You pick up enemies along the way. It's normal," she said, reproach in her tone, but he waited. "All right, I can irritate people. I've no patience with fools or varmints. A lot of people don't like me because I call things the way they are."

"Is that what you did with the Wranglers' Association?" he asked. "Call things the way they are?"

"Yes," Darcy Ingram said and gestured to a small sofa, barely more than a love seat. She handed him the coffee in a heavy mug as he sat down. Her breasts hardly moved as she sat down beside him, tucking her legs under her taut, compact body that had its own kind of attractiveness, a kind of contained energy. The words rose inside him, swam through his mind. *She wouldn't join. She's stubborn, thinks she's better than anybody else, full of crazy ideas of her own.* Carol's words about Darcy Ingram, and he turned them in his mind again as he cast a sidelong glance at her.

"How come you never joined up with the Wranglers' Association?" he asked casually.

"I'm against everything they are and everything they do. First, they cheat their buyers. They sell horses at three times a fair price. They agree between themselves to keep the prices up. The buyers think they're paying the going price. I won't do that. I sell my horses at a fair price and they're afraid of me for that. They know their customers will all start asking questions one of these days. That's why they want to get rid of me. They've tried other things before this."

"Then it's all competition," Fargo said.

"No, it's a lot more. I won't do what they will to bring in mustangs. Dave Cord will round up wild horses and then just shoot the ones he thinks are too old. He could let them go, just turn them loose, but that wouldn't satisfy his mean rottenness. I let a dozen of his older horses loose once and he's never forgiven me for that. Ed Buckley does the same thing and also sells horses he knows have problems that'll show up after they're sold. Marty Schotter will shoot a beautiful stallion, protecting his mares. The horses they do bring in they mistreat, breaking them, feeding them shit oats just good enough to fatten them for the drives."

"What about Carol Harwood?" Fargo questioned.

Darcy's eyes narrowed with new anger. "I think she's the worst," Darcy said.

"Why?"

"She goes along with everything the others do when she could change things."

"How?"

"She brought in new money when she came here. She could have used it to change things. I talked to her about it. She as much as told me to go to hell," Darcy said.

"So this is personal, besides," Fargo suggested.

"Everything is personal when you care about it," Darcy threw back. "I care about the wild horses I round up. I care about being fair with people. She doesn't. All she cares about is a chance to be as greedy as the others. She doesn't care a shit about the horses or cheating buyers with artificial prices. She could have made a difference. They'd have followed her. She's the big player now. I think when you've a chance to do something right and you don't do it, that makes you worse."

"How come they all stay in business?" Fargo queried.

"The buyers desperately want horses. I told you, they don't know they're being cheated by a conspiracy and I can only supply a few of them. But I'm going to make them all know it. I'm going to undersell them all even more than I do now," Darcy said.

"How?"

She leaned forward, excitement flooding her pugnaciously pretty face as her hand tightened on his arm. "What's the key to making money on the stock you sell?" she asked and didn't wait for an answer. "The key is how long you're on the trail. How many paydays do you have to spend on your hands. How many days can your stock eat range grass. Too many and you have to feed them oats out of your supply wagon. Oats cost money. Grass is free. The longer you're on the trail, the more chance you have of losing stock. There are always horses who go lame and founder on a long drive. There's always chance of a stampede or an Indian raid if you're a long time on the trail. If you can shorten your days on the trail you'll make more money on every horse or steer that you sell. I'm going to cut my trail time in half."

He smiled at the excitement in her face as she almost glowed. "Just how do you figure to do that?" he asked.

"I'm going to take my horses through the mountains," Darcy said with a flourish of triumph in her voice.

"You serious?" Fargo frowned.

"Absolutely. That's one of the reasons I asked you to come back. I want you to break trail for me through the mountains," she said.

He couldn't keep the rue from his half smile. "It won't work," he said.

"Yes, it will," Darcy returned firmly. "Why won't it?"

"For all kinds of reasons," Fargo said. "The mountains here aren't the Rockies but they're still mountains. You need open range to graze if you want to save oats, for one thing."

"There are high plateaus in the mountains," she said.

"None large enough. Besides, it's going onto October. The mountains reflect cold weather before the range," Fargo said. "Then you can't drive a herd through mountain passes. They're too narrow and dangerous."

"That's a misconception. The wild horses do it. They run through the passes all the time. I've seen them," Darcy said.

"Yes, but that's very different. They do it on their own, following their own instincts, obeying their own wisdoms. They're not being driven through. You can't compare it. There are a lot of other things.

You make a mistake on the range or something un-expected happens, you've room to correct it. The mountains won't let you make a mistake. The range will always challenge you, test you, but it'll give you a chance. The mountains won't."

"I say it can be done," Darcy snapped.

"Heard you were stubborn," Fargo said.

"From Carol Harwood. That's what she's always said because I won't go along with her and the oth-ers," Darcy shot back, and Fargo shrugged. "With you breaking trail, I know it can be done," Darcy said, her voice softening. "I'll pay you top dollar. Please, I need you. With Andy gone, I've nobody to help me."

"I am helping you. You're not listening," he said, not ungently.

She half pouted, her hand staying on his arm. "Think about it, please," she asked.

"Guess that won't hurt, if you'll do the same," he said.

"All right, it's a deal," Darcy agreed and rose with him as he finished the coffee and got to his feet. "If you're finished your visit with her, you can bed down here if you've a mind," she said.

"Haven't really finished yet," Fargo said.

"Don't let her tell you a lot of lies about me," Darcy said and suddenly sounded quite helpless. She was a strange mix, he decided, defiant, stubborn feistiness, and a little-girl appealingness. He'd not probe further for the moment, and when she walked outside with him she held his arm and again he felt the warm, firm, compactness of her. A half-dozen riders were driving some twenty mustangs into one of the corrals and he paused to watch. "They'll turn around a go after the rest," Darcy said. "I'm lucky. They didn't run off too far." Suddenly her head was against his chest, short brown hair soft against his face. "And I'm lucky you were near last night," she said. "Thank you, again." This time her lips brushed his cheek, slid to his mouth and lingered there, surprisingly soft and pliant. But she pulled away quickly. "Guess I'm feeling sorry for myself," she murmured.

"You've a right, seeing as what's happened," he said and pulled himself onto the pinto.

She nodded and he saw the pugnaciousness come into her face at once. "No goddamn rustlers," she hissed.

"We agree there," he said and rode from her. No rustlers, he repeated to himself as he put the Ovaro into a trot. But who? And why? The obvious answers were perhaps too obvious. But the enmity between Darcy and the others was very real and perhaps far from simple. The reasons were clear enough, competition, money, survival, power, plus the added element of female jealousy and bitchiness. The fury of women always had its own special edge, he had come to learn. Carol had always been ambitious and she was undoubtedly more so now. But ambition did not automatically lead to ruthlessness. Once again, the thought surfaced in his mind. How well did she know her associates? He grimaced at the thought that followed. Did she care what they might do? Looking the other way was often the easy solution.

Then there was Darcy Ingram. Time and place had drawn him into her problems. He felt sorry for her, he realized. She invited that with her combination of little-girl helplessness and stubborn, determined pugnaciousness. What else was in that strange mixture, he wondered. He turned the Ovaro south and skirted Carol's place as he followed Jeff Cotter's directions. He wanted more answers, a different perspective on Darcy. That called for a little more probing and he put the pinto into a fast trot as he saw the tall, wide-based pyramid-shaped rock.

3

The land beyond the pyramid-shaped rock rose in a slow incline, leveled off, and stayed mostly open but dotted with clusters of bitternut, with its preference for moist soil. The water came into sight soon after, a long ribbon of a river that ran swiftly and plentifully. Little sprays of white water cascaded into the air as it ran over rocks that seemed to run all through the river. The house rose up a few hundred yards in front of the water, low-roofed, stained a dark brown with small windows that gave it a dark and brooding air. He saw no stables, no barns, only two small sheds nearby. Fargo kept the Ovaro at a slow walk as he approached the house along the wide swatch of open land that ran past the structure to the water beyond. Peering at the house, he saw no sign of anyone when the shot exploded and he felt the whistle of it pass his head.

With a curse of surprise, he dove sideways from the saddle, hitting the ground as another two shots tore past him. He rolled, and when he glimpsed a stand of dense, four-foot tall wild radish, he flung himself into it. The tall, heavy-leafed woods gave way for him and instantly sprang back into place and he lay still and waited, but there were no further shots. The shooter also waited, uncertain of where he was in the line of tall weeds. Fargo lay still and finally lifted one hand to carefully part the tall leaves and peer across at the dark, brooding house. The shots had come from an open window in the front of the house, but the shooter was back inside the room and out of sight. Fargo drew his Colt, a precautionary move. "Sid Bundy?" he called. "Hold your fire."

The voice came from behind the open window. "Get out of here. You've got thirty seconds," it said.

"I didn't come for trouble, Bundy," Fargo said.

"Twenty-five seconds," the voice said, a grim implacableness in it.

"Just want to talk some," Fargo tried again.

"I don't talk with the likes of you. Twenty seconds," the man said.

"What's that supposed to mean?" Fargo asked.

"You're the one who saved that little bitch's neck. Eighteen seconds," the man said.

"How'd you know that, Bundy?" Fargo questioned.

"Got to town last night, I heard. They said you rode an Ovaro. Fifteen seconds."

Fargo cursed silently. "I'd have done it for anybody," he tried.

"Ten seconds," Sid Bundy's voice answered.

Fargo swore again. He had to know more about the man's hate. But his exchange had let Bundy zero in on where he was hidden in the weeds. Bundy would pour a volley into the spot. Some of the shots could well find their mark. "We can talk," Fargo said as he raised the Colt.

"Five seconds," Bundy rasped.

Fargo cursed. He'd lay down his own cover. He

46

pushed the Colt through the broad wild radish leaves and fired off three shots at the window, enough to keep Bundy off balance for a moment. A thin line of red ash ran along the side of the house. When his third shot resounded, he leaped up and burst from the weeds, his legs driving him toward the ash. Bundy's rifle fired, the first shot smashing into the ground at his heels. Fargo swerved and another shot tore past him. Swerving again, he felt the third shot go wide. But he had reached the ash and flung himself headlong into the trees, rolled, and came up on one knee against the light brown bark of a sapling. He peered at the house. The shooting had stopped and the furrow dug into Fargo's brow as he saw where the shots had landed. Bundy had fired them all from back of the one window and he hadn't moved to get a better angle as his target ran.

The furrow stayed on Fargo's brow as he rose and on silent steps made his way through the trees along the side of the house. He halted when he spotted the buckboard a few feet from the rear of the house. The wagon had something he'd never seen on a buckboard, an extra iron handgrip that went down along the side of the open seat. There was one on each side, he noted as he moved on until he halted across from a rear door in the house. Bundy had no doubt moved from the window by now, Fargo surmised. He waited somewhere inside.

The rear door beckoned and he decided to run for it. He drove himself across the open ground but pulled up sharply just as he reached the door. Fargo dropped, almost flattening himself on the ground as he realized that Bundy could be canny enough to anticipate he'd find the rear door. Staying low, Fargo reached out one hand slowly and carefully turned the doorknob. He felt it click open and pulled his hand back. He raised his left leg and drew it back, the Colt gripped in one hand, and kicked it out with all his strength. The door flew open and the rifle shots exploded instantly, two fired in quick succession, and Fargo felt them whistle over his head. Had he been standing at the door, both shots would have smashed into him. He rose, the Colt aimed point-blank at the man just inside the door. "Drop the rifle," he said as he felt the wave of astonishment sweep over him. "Goddamn," he breathed. "Never shot a man in a wheelchair. Don't make this a first."

Sid Bundy eyed the Colt, saw it couldn't miss, and slowly let the rifle slide from his hands. Fargo straightened up as he moved forward. He stepped through the doorway and frowned at the man in the wheelchair. He saw a strong-boned face, glowering, dark eyes, and short-cut black hair, a face that flung back bitter defiance. "Finished being surprised?" the man spit out.

"No," Fargo said honestly. "You tried to kill me, goddammit. That wheelchair's no excuse."

"I gave you thirty seconds to leave," Sid Bundy answered.

Fargo's gaze took in the wheelchair again. "Now I understand the extra iron grips on the buckboard," he said. "You can get out of that chair."

"With my canes," the man said, hate in his eyes.

"All this because I helped Darcy Ingram?"

"Goddamn right," the man shot back.

"Why? What's this all about?" Fargo questioned.

"This is what it's about, this goddamn wheelchair. She put me here," Bundy said, his voice rising and his hands clenching on the arms of the chair. Fargo stared at the man, saw his lips quiver in fury, his face consume itself with hate. "She doesn't deserve saving, not that little bitch," Bundy rasped.

There was no questioning the man's fury, Fargo saw. "How'd she put you in that wheelchair? Tell me about it," Fargo said calmly. Bundy licked his lips as he reined in his outburst.

"Why not? It was two years ago this week. I keep living it over and over. Why not tell it," Sid Bundy said, as much to himself as his listener. "I won't ever be forgetting it. I can't," he grunted with wry bitterness. "Of course, it all started when she wanted to bring her herd to my water."

"She wanted you to let her water her herd as a favor?" Fargo questioned.

"I don't do favors," Bundy growled. "She knew she was going to have to pay. I wasn't much for the idea. I've my own uses for the river. But she kept at me, raising her offer each time."

"You agree, finally?" Fargo asked.

"Yes, but I wasn't happy about it. We do a lot of trapping and fishing along the river. I still didn't like the idea of a bunch of mustangs running all over my land," Bundy said. "I changed my mind the day before she was to make her first trip to the water. I sent word to her not to come, had one of my men tell her I'd called off the deal. I figured that was the end of it. I was wrong."

"Meaning what?"

"The next morning I'm at the river with four of my men. We're testing out new traplines and lures. Suddenly I hear the horses, the whole goddamn herd of them coming at us. We jumped up, but they were galloping all out to get to the water. We yelled and waved at them but they just kept coming. We tried to run but it was too late. They spread out, kept charging, and stampeded right over us. I was the luckiest. I had both legs broken but I'm still alive. The others were killed."

"You think Darcy sent them on purpose," Fargo probed.

"Goddamn right. She ignored my message, wanted to push her way through, probably figured once the horses were there it'd be past changing. Goddamn bitch," Bundy flared again.

"Maybe she never got the message," Fargo suggested.

Bundy's lips curled in derision. "That's what she said, only I know she got it. There was a witness with my man when he delivered it."

"Who?" Fargo asked.

"Dave Cord."

"From the association?"

"He knew my man and rode along with him. Thank God for that much, but I'm still a cripple because of her, goddamn her," Bundy said.

"It's time she paid for that, right?" Fargo slid at the man.

"Way past time," Bundy said.

"You've been wanting to pay her back ever since, think about it all the time," Fargo said.

"Every damn minute." Bundy snarled.

Fargo let thoughts churn through his mind for a moment. Was Sid Bundy behind the attack on Darcy? He was filled with the kind of bitter hate that fermented until revenge became an obsession. Hiring attackers wouldn't have been a problem. There were always men waiting who'd do anything for money. But Fargo wanted to hear more. Bundy had painted a Darcy Ingram of total disregard for honor, human life, for anything but what she wanted. Darcy was stubborn, plainly a young woman determined to have her way. That was evident enough. But was she coldly ruthless? Fargo wanted to know more before he'd accept that. Besides, Dave Cord as a witness was a question mark of its own. Fargo's eyes focused on Sid Bundy's burning glare.

"All this doesn't give you leave to try and kill me, Bundy," Fargo said, but he saw no remorse in the man's face. "Don't ever try it again, wheelchair or no wheelchair." Bundy didn't answer and Fargo backed out the door. He was about to turn when he caught the movement of Bundy's upper body and saw his hand reach down to bring up the rifle in a scooping motion. The Colt flew into Fargo's hand, fired a single shot that hit the rifle just behind the rear sight and sent it skittering into the air. "You really want to be a first time?" Fargo frowned, the Colt ready to fire again. Bundy eyed the pistol and his angry scowl gave way to the grudging realization that this big man was not given to idle threats.

He slumped in the wheelchair, the rifle out of easy reach, and Fargo turned and strode away. He pulled himself onto the Ovaro and rode away at a fast trot, anxious to be gone from a place drenched in bitter hate. He made his way back to Darcy's place in the fading hours of the day, and reached it to see the corrals filled with horses. She came from the cabin to meet him, triumph in her determined face. "Got most all of them rounded up and back," she said.

"Good for you," he said, swinging to the ground.

"I'll be driving the herd in a day or two," Darcy said.

"Through the mountains?" he asked.

"Yes. Haven't changed my mind on that."

"Neither have I," he said.

"It can be done, especially if you'll break trail for me," Darcy said with sudden vehemence. "Please go with me."

"Met somebody," he said, ignoring her plea. "Definitely not one of your admirers."

"That takes in a lot of people, most of the town," Darcy said with a sniff.

"Sid Bundy," he said and saw her face tighten.

"I know what he told you, heard it often enough," she said with a sneer in her voice. "A lie's a lie, no matter how many times you tell it."

"That's true but he's in a wheelchair. No lie about that," Fargo said.

"That's the only truth," she snapped.

"I'm listening," he said.

"It was agreed I could drive my horses to his water. That's what I did," Darcy said.

"He sent word to you he'd called off the agreement," Fargo said.

"There was no word. Nobody told me anything and I sent the herd. I was with them, pulling up at the rear. I didn't even see Bundy and his men by the water until it was too late."

"Bundy says you were told. There was a witness," Fargo pushed at her.

"Dave Cord. Some witness," she spit out derisively. "It was all set up to get at me, make me look as though I'd ignored the message, make me into a cold, rotten bitch who'd do anything to get her way."

"Which still makes it one word against two, yours against Bundy's man and Dave Cord," Fargo said.

"That's right. They planned it well. They used Bundy, made a pawn out of him. They didn't figure on his being trampled and others killed. That became a bonus for them, but they had it all set up. He was paid to call off our agreement."

"How do you know that?" Fargo questioned.

"Sid Bundy didn't have any money to speak of but his doctor bills were paid in full. I asked Doc Everest about that. The doc told me Sid Bundy said he could pay his bills because the association paid him for something he did for them. He did something all right, took part in setting me up. It just backfired on him."

"Even if you're right, you've no proof," Fargo said.

"I've more. How do you think Bundy's been living since that time?" Darcy asked. "He can't trap, fish, farm, do odd jobs."

"Don't know. Takes in an occasional boarder?" Fargo shrugged.

"I wondered about that and I watched, waited. Once a month, Dave Cord visits him in the dead of night with an envelope of money, same time, same night, every month. What do you think that money's for? Because they're so kindhearted?"

"They're buying his silence," Fargo said.

"Go to the head of the class," Darcy snapped.

"You tell anybody?" Fargo asked.

"Who'd believe me? Not the good Sheriff Bailey. They own him. It'd be more of the same, their word against mine. But that's the truth of it, believe me or not," Darcy said.

"I can believe you. Dave Cord as a witness seemed damn convenient to me," Fargo said.

"They figured with the whole town mostly turned against me I'd pack up and leave. But I didn't. I even got a few folks to give me the benefit of the doubt. It didn't work for them. They didn't force me to leave. Now they're afraid I'll really put them out of business by going through the mountains. The fire was another try at getting rid of me once and for all," Darcy said.

"You keep thinking it had to be the association. Bundy could have been behind it. He hates you enough," Fargo said.

"I guess so, but he's into brooding and hating, everyone and everything, including himself. He's not into acting on it," Darcy said.

"Don't be too sure," Fargo said.

"You said you could believe me. Does that mean you'll come with me?" Darcy said, the little-girl part of her rushing forward in her again, needing, pleading, reaching out with an explosion of warmth.

"For only one reason," Fargo said, and she waited, frowning. "I'll go to show you it can't be done. I'll go to help you get out of this alive."

"Deal. I'll settle for that," she said instantly and threw her arms around him in a quick hug, and he felt the compactness of her. "Will you stay for supper?" she asked, stepping back.

"Can't," he said.

"Carol Harwood?" she queried with a sidelong glance.

"We're old friends, I told you. We've old times to talk about. Besides, I want to stop in town. The Ovaro's got a loose shoe. I want to visit the smithy."

"See you tomorrow?"

"Count on it," Fargo said.

She came to him again, her arms encircling his neck. "I know you're old friends with her but don't let her turn you against me. She's smart and very smooth," Darcy said. "She's said a lot of things about me to others."

"I listen, always, but I make up my own mind," Fargo said.

"Good," Darcy said, and her lips brushed his cheek, a quick, light touch as the tips of her breasts came against him for an instant. "You won't be sorry you're helping me. Maybe you being at the right place at the right time was a kind of sign."

"Of what?"

"I'm not sure," she said, a tiny smile edging her full lips. "I guess we'll be finding that out."

She stepped back and he pulled himself onto the Ovaro and rode away as she waved him off. He put the horse into an easy gait and the night had descended when he reached Carol's place. The house was dark, with only a candle burning in the front window, and Jeff Cotter came by carrying a sack of feed. "She hasn't come back yet. It happens. Buyers can take their own sweet time," Cotter said.

"If she does arrive, tell her I'll be back," he said, and sent the horse into a slow trot. His thoughts found their way back to Darcy. Her explanations had been convincing, almost completely, yet an edge of dissatisfaction pushed at him. She'd not really fought back and that was out of character for her. She considered the sheriff a bought man yet she could have flung what she had learned at him, fought back, made her own demands for answers.

But she hadn't. She'd been content to keep what she'd seen to herself. It just didn't fit the kind of determination he'd seen in her.

He believed her, yet he realized that all he had was words, her words, her explanations. And his own gut feelings. But words and feelings could betray. He had learned that lesson long ago. He wanted something more, even only an indication, an affirmation. His thoughts were still idling when he rode into Foxville and moved through the darkened streets to the oasis of light in the center of town. There were no better sources of information in a town than bartenders and madams. Everything sooner or later came their way and experience taught them how to sort out the truth, how to sift through gossip to find reality. He dismounted before the saloon and noted the sign: BOTTLE, BEEF, AND BED. Hitching the Ovaro to the post, Fargo went inside and his eyes swept a bar well filled with customers, a large room with round tables that were mostly filled.

A woman came toward him at once, clothed in a tight red dress and using a red boa to partially cover voluminous breasts that spilled over a low-cut neckline. Tight peroxide-blond curls framed a wide, pleasant face that was still attractive despite the years on it. "Welcome, big man," she said. "I'm Lola. Your first visit here?" Fargo returned a nod as a younger woman appeared in a black waitress outfit that revealed plenty of leg and a skimpy top. Tall, she was pretty enough despite a hardness in her blue eyes. "This is Inez," Lola said. "She'll take care of anything you want."

"Beef and bourbon," Fargo said, sliding into a chair at the nearest table.

"That's a good start. Maybe you'll go on from there." Lola smiled broadly.

"Maybe," he allowed.

"Staying in town a spell?" the madam asked as Inez hurried away to fill his order.

He took a moment and chose words. "Came on a visit, wound up getting into a rescue," he said, and Lola's eyes widened instantly.

"You the one who saved Darcy Ingram?" she asked, and he allowed a modest smile.

"Afraid so. It sure wasn't popular with everybody," he said, putting rueful surprise into his voice.

"I'd guess not," Lola said as Inez brought the bourbon. "There are a lot who don't like Darcy Ingram."

"Why?" Fargo queried quickly. "You know her?" he added with more casualness.

"Mostly from what I hear. Met her a few times. She's sure no customer," the madam said.

"What do you hear?"

"She the righteous kind, no give in her and she won't back down. She fights. She thinks that's how to get her way," Lola said with a touch of disdain.

"You don't agree with that," Fargo said.

"You get more flies with honey than vinegar." Lola sniffed.

"The Wranglers' Association, they customers?" Fargo questioned.

"From time to time. Except for Carol Harwood, of course."

"What do you know about her?" Fargo pressed.

"She's real sharp. She doesn't look down her nose at folks the way Darcy Ingram does. And she doesn't try to bull her way. She's too smart for that. But she gets what she wants. I'm not for crossing her," the madam said.

He gave Lola a sidelong glance. "I get the feeling you don't much like either of them," he said.

"Bull's-eye." Lola laughed. "One's too self-righteous and pigheaded, the other's too clever."

Fargo allowed a wry smile. The madam knew how to read people. It was basic to her existence. She had affirmed some things for him, reinforced others he had already concluded. But he wanted more brought to the surface and decided to stir the pot further. Lola was the perfect vehicle. Spreading tidbits and gossip was almost a second vocation for madams. It gave them a dash of status in a position that was pretty low on status. "I still figure to give Darcy a hand," he said casually. "She wants me to take her herd across the mountains. I'll do it. I feel sorry for her."

He saw Lola digest the announcement. "You'll be getting a medal for good deeds," Lola said as she hurried away. It would be all over town come morning, he knew, and he sat back as Inez brought a hearty beef sandwich smothered with gravy. "Call for me if you decide to stay longer," Inez said, a reticent quality in her.

"I'll do that, Inez," Fargo said. "You been here long?"

"Not very," the girl said, two words that explained so much, and he watched her walk away on nice slender legs encased in black net stockings. She had a sweetness to her that hadn't yet been rubbed away. He ate slowly and watched the saloon gather in new customers. He rose from the table when he finished and Lola detached herself from the bar when he started for the door.

"Be waiting for your next visit," she called out.

"What makes you sure I'll be coming back?" He smiled.

"I'm guessing you're not finished asking questions," the woman said, and he chuckled as he strode from the saloon.

Lola embodied the wisdom of her world, a place of gut experiences that provided an unvarnished reality. Outside, he unhitched the Ovaro and rode back to Carol's place, where the lone candle was still the only light. He went into the bedroom after stabling the Ovaro, undressed, and stretched out. Carol had still not returned when he finally fell asleep. He woke with the morning sun streaming into the room, alone in the bed. When he was dressed, he found that Maria had coffee and bacon waiting in the kitchen. He had just finished the meal when he heard the hoofbeats and went to the door to see Carol skidding the horse to a halt and almost jumping from the saddle. She strode toward him, hazel eyes flashing, her face drawn tight.

"Welcome back," Fargo said. "Took you longer than you expected."

"Is it true?" Carol flung at him, ignoring his greeting.

"Is what true?" Fargo frowned.

"I stopped in town. Word's out that you're taking Darcy through the mountains. Is it true?" she demanded icily.

"In a way," he said.

"Get out," Carol spit at him, fury wreathing her face. "Get out now."

"She asked me for help. I felt sorry for her. She's going to need help," Fargo said.

"I offered you a job helping me," Carol flung back.

"You don't need help. You're driving your herd with the others. You've plenty of help," he said. "Besides, it's not that simple. Somebody tried to kill her and all her horses."

"Rustlers."

"I don't buy that."

"You don't want to buy it. You'd rather play the big rescuer. Did she promise to screw you?" Carol threw at him.

"You're way off base," Fargo said.

"Am I? You want to help her, then go ahead. But you're not helping her from my bed. Get out, dammit," Carol almost screamed.

"We'll talk after you calm down," Fargo tried.

"I won't be calming down," Carol said, and he shrugged as he walked from the house, the door slamming behind him. She was too furious to listen or reason with and he decided to let the fury subside in her. He went to the stable, saddled the Ovaro, and looked for her as he rode away, but she was closeted inside the house. Her rage had surprised him. He was to blame for some of it, he realized. Old-fashioned jealousy played a part in it. But what else? There was almost a sense of fear in her fury. For herself, or for others in the Wranglers' Association? Did she inwardly believe more than she dared to admit, even to herself. Or were there things she knew, demons she had to wrestle with inside herself?

The questions circled inside him. She'd not be easy to reach. Carol's passion ran too deep, too consuming, under bedcovers or outside them. Only his backing away from Darcy would satisfy her. Perhaps he could still talk sense into Darcy, he contemplated as he rode into town. He'd try again, he told himself, and the thought took on immediacy as Darcy appeared on a piebald mustang. She saw him at the same time he did her, and spurred the horse toward him. He saw her full lips were drawn into a thin line as she came to a halt. "I was on my way to see you," he said.

"Don't bother," she snapped.

"Why? What's the matter?" he frowned.

"I'm not having a wolf herd sheep," she said, icy reproach in her voice.

"What are you talking about?" he questioned, feeling the irritation push at him.

"You lied to me. You're not just old friends with her. You've been staying the nights at her place. 'We've a lot of old times to talk over,'" she said in a mocking echo of his words. "Try a lot of old times to fuck over."

His eyes hardened. "You shouldn't be listening to everything you hear and it's none of your business," he said.

"Hands know what they know and it is my business. I told you what they were like. Nobody rides with me who's all cozy with them," Darcy flung back.

"She's not like the others," Fargo protested. "I told you that."

"And I told you she's worse. I guess there's screwing and there's seeing. The one gets in the way of the other," Darcy said, self-righteousness in her anger. "I don't want your help, not anymore."

"You're going to need it," Fargo said.

"No, I won't. I don't want help from anybody screwing her," Darcy said.

He felt irritation turning to anger at her stubborn shortsightedness. She was trading reason for emotion, commonsense for bitchiness. "You sound jealous," he tossed at her and saw her eyes grow darker.

"I'm not jealous and I don't care how I sound. Just don't help me anymore, understand?" she threw back.

"Understand," he snapped angrily, spurring the Ovaro forward and brushing past her at a canter. He held the pace, steering around spring wagons and buckboards, slowing only when he reached the end of town. Feelings had crystallized inside him, he realized. Carol could keep her jealous wounds, Darcy could cling to her ungrateful bitchiness. They were both driven by their own agendas, Carol by her consuming pursuit of the dollar, Darcy by her almost missionary zeal to right a wrong. Both had turned their backs on him, one with icy disdain, the other with ungrateful stubbornness. The hell with both of them. He could indulge his own self-righteousness, he muttered.

He started to walk the Ovaro forward when he heard the hoofbeats coming up behind him. Turning to see the three riders, he recognized Dave Cord first, then Ed Buckley's beefy form and Marty Schotter's long, angular build, sticklike atop a dark roan. "Been looking for you, Fargo," Dave Cord called out. "We're real unhappy with what we've heard."

"What might that be?" Fargo answered quietly.

"Word is you're taking Darcy Ingram through the mountains," the man said.

Fargo grunted wryly and decided he'd say nothing about Darcy changing her mind. "She asked if I'd help her," he said.

"That wouldn't be a good idea," Ed Buckley said.

Fargo kept his face bland, but he felt the instant resentment gathering inside him. "Meaning what exactly?" he said.

"Let her go on her own," Cord said. "She'll never make it."

"But she might with you taking her through," Marty Schotter said. "We don't want that. Butt out, Fargo."

"If I don't?" Fargo inquired mildly.

"You could be real sorry," Dave Cord answered.

Fargo's slow smile was edged with ice. "Now, that sounds awfully much like a threat," he said.

"Let's call it advice," Cord said with a growl.

"Advice wrapped in a threat," Fargo said, his tone hardening. The three men shrugged wordlessly, letting the coldness in their eyes answer. Fargo gave a long sigh. "I don't much like being threatened, gents. It kind of makes my back all stiff. Sometimes it makes me mad enough to kick ass. In fact, I feel that coming over me right now, so I'd suggest you hightail it real fast."

Dave Cord swallowed hard, his eyes going to where Fargo's hand rested on the butt of the Colt. The other two men followed as he wheeled his horse and rode away at a fast trot. "You'll be sorry," Ed Buckley called back, and Fargo waited till they were out of sight before he moved the Ovaro forward. The meeting stuck inside him, reinforcing his suspicions about the men. Would they try to insure that Darcy didn't make it through the mountains? The odds weren't good for Darcy. He swore softly as he realized his own self-righteousness had just been shattered. Walking away was suddenly a lot harder, maybe too hard.

4

Fargo rode slowly, staying in the cottonwoods, and eventually found himself skirting the charred remains of Darcy's place. Peering through the trees, he saw her beside the corrals with some of her hands, while others worked with the mustangs inside. He watched as a young cowhand filled leather sacks with oats under Darcy's supervision. Fargo grunted in grim approval. She had plainly decided against taking extra oats by wagon and was clearly preparing to carry them on packhorses. But he frowned as he saw the cowhand carry off the filled sacks, tying each, and he watched for her to order others filled. But she didn't and this time his grunt was made of disapproval. She was taking too few oats, he noted. But it was plain that she'd be ready to move the herd in another day or two. Keeping to the trees, he rode on, leaving the scene behind and cutting across land dotted with stands of burr oak.

The glint of sun or water caught his eye and he followed it to a lake, mostly round but with an irregular-shaped shoreline and heavily bordered with black willow, pecan, and shagbark hickory. He halted, listened, and heard only the sound of yellow warblers, orioles, and meadowlarks, all good, reassuring sounds that told of peaceful, easy surroundings. He eased the horse forward and halted again at the edge of the lake, where two thick black willows pushed their branches over the water. Swinging from the Ovaro, he pulled off his clothes, the lake inviting in the still-warm September day. It was a perfect spot for quiet reflection, for enjoying the best of nature's gifts. Putting his Colt and gunbelt in a neat pile at the edge of the shore, he sank into the lake as the Ovaro moved under the long leaves of a pecan tree to graze. He let the cool water flow around his muscled body, lazily swimming from the shore. He noted a large piece of broken tree trunk floating almost in the center of the lake.

He turned on his back and dove under the water, swimming among the long, thin stems of water shamrock and the heavier tendrils of underwater marshes. Rising to the surface, he played in the water, then floated peacefully, his arms behind his head. Time seemed to vanish and he drifted to the shore at a spot where he relaxed half in and half out of the water as the sun filtered down through the long, narrow leaves of a black willow. But thoughts had their own way of persisting, of quietly nudging one, he found, refusing to let even quietude turn them off. The exchange with Dave Cord, Buckley, and Marty Schotter refused to go away. It stayed lodged inside him, not unlike a piece of chicken bone in his gullet. It also left him with a rush of newly ambivalent feelings about Darcy.

She'd been toweringly ungrateful and stubborn, putting her hurt feelings over everything else. Like a recalcitrant, uncooperative child, she deserved to pay for her attitude. But paying was one thing. Dying was another, he grimaced. How much of Dave Cord and the others was bluster and hollow threat, he wondered. The fire instantly leaped in his thoughts. There had been no hollow bluster about that. But were they behind it? There was still Sid Bundy. He was unwilling to dismiss the man as cavalierly as Darcy did. And were there others Darcy had made into bitter enemies? The questions floated in his thoughts as lazily as he floated in the lake. Perhaps he'd be doing Darcy a favor by letting her fail on her own. It might well prove to her the idea was a bad one. Failure has a way of teaching its own lessons. But was failure all that would happen to her, he grimaced. Even without the shadowy presence of Cord, Bundy, and the others, the mountains could easily bring the ultimate failure, death.

Was he being too dramatic, too concerned, he pondered. Dave Cord and the others had left him, convinced he was going to help Darcy. Perhaps that was enough to make them back off. Perhaps, he swore silently. And then, off by herself, there was Carol. Was she involved or not involved, removed or not removed. How much did she know? Or how little? Was she a part of it, by looking away, or was she innocent of anything but ambition and jealousy? He drew a grim sigh and noticed the sun slipping behind the mountains to the north. The hours of lazy relaxing and unanswered questions had too quickly slipped away. He stretched in the water when he heard the sound, a whinny from the Ovaro.

It was not the whinny of greeting, of relaxed, idle pleasure. This was the whinny of alarm, sudden, tense tightness in it. He knew the Ovaro's many voices as well as he knew his own, that close communication that was part of oneness, of trust and bonding. He felt his body grow tight at once and brought the lower part of his torso down to straighten in the water so that he stood upright, head and chest exposed. He began to half walk, half swim in the shallow water, moving along the shoreline toward where he had left his clothes and Colt. He was almost there when the rider came from the black willows, staying in the saddle and halting but a few feet from where the Colt lay in its gunbelt at the edge of the lake. The man saw Fargo at once and Fargo watched a slack-jawed face take on a satisfied sneer. "Come on out, mister," the man invited.

Fargo didn't move and saw two more riders appear and come to a halt at the edge of the lake. In moments, two others rode from the trees a few feet to the left. Five in all, Fargo counted as his eyes returned to the slack-jawed one. "You just wandering by?" Fargo asked.

"Wandering, looking, finding, no matter to you," the man said.

"It could be," Fargo said.

"Not anymore," the man said, his sneering grin widening as his eyes moved over Fargo's muscled torso. "Looks like you're going to leave this world the same way you came into it," he said and drew a laugh from one of the others. Fargo's eyes swept the men and their cold faces and hard eyes, worn gunbelts and shabby clothes. Drifters, he grunted, dangerous men because they had nothing to lose and nothing to love. Fargo's gaze left the men and glanced at the lake. The sun had gone behind the distant mountains. Fargo guessed there was fifteen minutes to go before complete darkness descended. He had to survive till then to have any chance of staying alive, fifteen minutes was suddenly a euphemism for eternity. There was no time for further thoughts about the five men. There was time to think only about harboring minutes to stay alive. His eyes scanned the lake again. In many places, the willows edged the shore to stretch branches over the water and his glance went to the log in the center of the lake. When he returned his gaze to the shore, he saw the slack-jawed figure reaching for his gun.

"Let him have it," the man suddenly snarled to the others. Fargo gulped in a deep breath, sank underwater, and kicked his feet hard as he swam to the bottom. He leveled off in the shallow water and could hear the gunfire that sounded strangely muffled. Keeping to the shoreline, he stayed underwater till he felt the last of his breath disappear. He streaked upward, his head pushing out of the water as he drew in deep gulps of air. He heard the hoofbeats at once and turned to see one horseman racing along the edge of the lake toward him. But others were galloping in the other direction along the shore. Unable to spot him underwater, they had smartly decided to cover the shoreline in both directions. Cursing, he drew in breath and sank underwater again as he heard the spraying sound of the water where bullets struck just to his right. He struck out again, staying underwater near the shore until his lungs forced him to surface once more.

Head cutting the water, he blinked and saw that he was halfway around the lake. But he also saw his attackers had spread out all around the lake, one or another ready for wherever he might try to go ashore. The night was closing fast, he saw. But he wasn't the only one to realize that as a volley of bullets erupted, the shots hitting the water on both sides of him. With another quick glance at the log in the center of the lake, he filled his lungs with air and dove underwater, swimming furiously at once as more shots struck the water. When he had to surface again, he rose and saw that he had guessed well, the log only a half foot from him in the fast-fading light. He drew in air, reached out, and clung to the log as he refilled his lungs. But they had been waiting, straining their eyes in the last of the light, and he heard their shouts as they saw him.

"There he is," one shouted. "By the log."

"Kill him, dammit," Fargo heard the slack-jawed man shout and he saw them all pull rifles from saddle cases. Staying beside the log, he sank below the surface as the rifle fire erupted, the heavier bullets smashing into the log as well as the water. They were firing from three sides of the lake and Fargo cursed as he saw they were bracketing the log, drawing their fire inward. A shot smashed into the log just above his head, putting a hole through the rotted wood from one side to the other. He sank down further and his lips drew back, his mouth almost filling with water as a shot struck him, a grazing blow along his upper arm. He felt another bullet plow a path through the water and graze his forehead. He had to do something, he realized. They were doing too good a job of bracketing their gunfire and at the next shot, he pushed upward. "There, get him," the shout rose at once. Fargo pushed himself backward as another volley of bullets hit on both sides of him.

But this time he bellowed a curse of pain, followed the next shot with a sharper cry. Flailing the water with one arm, he made a gargling sound as he disappeared below the surface. "I think we got him," he heard one of the men shout. Staying beneath the log, he waited as long as he could and only when it seemed his chest was about to burst, did he come up for air. Pushing only the top of his head through the surface of the water, he pressed his lips against the hole that had been shot through the log and sucked in air through it. Darkness had fallen, he saw with relief as he filled his lungs. Staying with his lips pressed to the hole in the log, he listened, heard the scrape of rein chains, then the sound of a horse blowing air and moments after, the soft slap of saddle leather rubbed against a stirrup. The five horses were still spread around the edges of the lake, the riders still in place, still waiting. As if in confirmation, another of the horses pawed the ground, further off to his left. Fargo continued to listen until he had three of the men placed in his mind, when a fourth one finished the task for him.

"Let's go, he's done for," the man said from directly across where the log floated.

"Shut up and keep your eyes open," a voice answered in a coarse whisper, and Fargo smiled. He had the last two in place, one just to his right. Taking his mouth from the hole in the log, Fargo let himself slide silently under the surface and began to swim underwater with slow, silent strokes. When the last of the air gave out in his lungs, he floated upward, being careful not to cause as much as a ripple in the water. Treading water, he peered forward, where the faintest glint of the rising moon intruded on the pitch blackness. He slid through the water silent as a copperhead, reaching the shore where a big black willow hung its branches over the water.

He halted under the overhanging tree. He could see the dark bulk of the nearest horseman, some fifteen feet away, standing at the water's edge. Fargo floated in place as he surveyed the scene. The water would almost certainly lap up onto the shore when he emerged, no matter how careful he was. The horseman was near enough to hear that, Fargo knew. He couldn't risk that. The water had to stay its still, almost motionless self, a silent ally not a soft alarm. Reaching up with both hands, he grasped the willow branch, lifted himself slowly, using all the strength and muscle he had. He pulled himself straight upward, his long body rising out of the water, leaving not even a ripple behind. He hung on the branch for a moment, then pulled himself along its length until he was over the shoreline. Opening his hands, he let himself drop noiselessly onto the soft, moist soil. He paused to take in deep drafts of air, then moved forward in a crouch. In his nakedness, he felt not unlike the primitive hunter of eons ago, without clothes, weapons, armed only with guile and speed, approaching a more dangerous and more powerful target.

Like that ancient, primitive hunter, he would have but one chance. Failure meant death. The pages of time seemed to turn backward as moving on the balls of his feet in the soft soil, he was a silent, unseen figure. The man astride the horse, one hand on the butt of his gun in its holster, peered across the lake. It was his horse that sensed the naked figure moving closer. The animal moved and blew air through its nostrils. "Whoa, dammit," the man hissed. They were his last words. Fargo, almost at the horse's side, propelled himself upward, turning his powerful legs into springs.

He clasped one hand over the man's mouth while with his other hand he yanked the man's head in a half circle. He felt the crack of vertebrae and the figure went limp, toppled from the saddle into his arms.

The horse bolted, the instant of silence shattered. Fargo heard the nearest rider wheel his horse and shout. On one knee, Fargo yanked the man's gun from its holster, saw that it was an Allen and Wheelock single-action army revolver. It would shoot high and pull to the right. They always did, he grunted as he prepared to adjust for it. The horseman was racing down at him, another following a dozen yards behind. Fargo took aim, fired the pistol, and the figure in the saddle jerked before toppling from the horse. The next rider, moving faster, was close behind, and Fargo was able to see his slack-jawed face. The man fired as he charged, his shots too high and, again adjusting for the revolver, Fargo fired again. The man pitched forward atop his horse before sliding lifelessly from the saddle. Fargo spun, staying crouched, as he heard the hoofbeats from the other side of the lake. He was ready, the gun aimed, as the rider became more than an onrushing black bulk. Firing a single shot, Fargo saw the rider go backward over his horse's rump. He was ready to fire again when the last horseman reined up, spun his horse, and galloped away. Fargo waited till the last fleeing hoofbeat had died away before he rose, dropped the gun distastefully, and walked to where his clothes and his Colt lay on the ground.

He reached the spot, pulled on his clothes and gunbelt, and whistled. The Ovaro came in moments, materializing out of the darkness, and as Fargo pulled himself onto the horse he felt the warm liquid running down his arm and sliding along his temple. He felt with his fingers and realized he had not come away untouched and remembered the shots that had grazed him in the water. He turned the horse from the lake and felt the moment of dizziness pass through him and was not surprised. The need to survive brought its own desperate demands. It took over the body and the mind, calling on every ounce of physical and mental concentration. When the consuming need passed, nature asserted itself, rushing forward with its own demands. He grimaced at newfound pain as he realized he had to stop himself from losing too much blood. Carol's place was nearest and he put the pinto into a slow trot.

It was not a destination he'd have chosen but perhaps, in its own way, it was as good as any. His upper arm hurt and he could feel the blood still running, soaking his shirtsleeve. He fought away another wave of dizziness and was glad for the Ovaro's smooth gait. Carol's place was dark when he reached it. He reined to a halt, slid from the horse, and the front door opened at his touch. "You home?" he called as he went inside where a small night candle burned. A lamp went on in the bedroom and Carol came out and put on another lamp. Her eyes widened at him.

"My God, what happened to you?" she asked, setting the lamp down.

"Need some bandage cloths," he said. She hurried away as he carefully pulled his shirt off, and soon returned with cloths and a washbasin of warm water. She wore a blue nightgown, he saw, and her longish breasts swayed beautifully as she began to wash the blood from his arm and chest.

"Talk," she said as she examined the long, scraping

wound on his arm and began to wrap the bandage cloths around it.

"Let's start with your friends," Fargo said and told her of his meeting with Dave Cord and the other two men, followed with the attack at the lake. She had just cleaned the blood from his temple when he finished and she stepped back.

"You connecting the two things?" She frowned.

"You're damn right," Fargo snapped.

"You're wrong," Carol said. "I can see Dave Cord trying to scare you off of helping Darcy. He'd do something dumb like that, but that's all he'd do. The men at the lake were common highwaymen."

"Highwaymen who didn't take an expensive rifle, a hand-tooled Colt, and a fine saddle? Highwaymen who waited around to kill me when they could've grabbed things and ran? Bullshit, honey. They had orders," Fargo said.

"Not from the association," Carol said. "You certainly don't think I'd have anything to do with something like that, do you?"

"I'm trying not to. It's getting harder," Fargo returned.

She let one perpetually raised brow lift further. "Because I'm being loyal to my friends?"

"There's loyal and there's blind," Fargo said, and she glowered back and managed to look beautiful doing it. "You want me to believe you? You want me to believe they didn't send those varmints looking for me? Prove it. Give me somebody else."

"I'll try," she said.

"I'll come for answers," he warned.

"I'll try," she repeated. "Look for me on the range. We'll be driving our horses east come tomorrow." She came closer and put both hands on his chest. "I'm sorry for what happened. You could still come with us."

"Not till I know who I'm riding with," he said. "Thanks for the bandaging." She brought her mouth to his, her breasts soft against his chest. "I could stay," he said.

"Not till I know who you're screwing," she said.

"You've a suspicious nature," he said.

"Look who's talking," she said. He stepped back and walked to the door, and she turned away only when he left. Outside, he climbed onto the Ovaro, favoring his sore arm, and rode till he found a glen in a stand of burr oak. He set out his bedroll and decided two things before he slept. Carol was still a question mark and he couldn't just walk away from Darcy. A conscience was a pain in the ass, he muttered.

5

Fargo watched from between the tall, red-hued sandstone rocks. He waited patiently, certain it was the way she would come. Earlier in the morning he'd paused to watch Carol and the others begin to move their combined herds across the range. Dave Cord and Marty Schotter rode near her, he noted, but she kept to herself. The cowhands moved the large herd slowly, careful not to upset horses unused to each other. They knew their job, Fargo noted. Finally he'd turned away and rode north to the mountains. A wide slope beckoned invitingly. He took it even as he knew it was a delusion, nature's way of casting out a lure and he knew Darcy would take it.

The day had slid into midmorning when she proved him right as she came into sight at the front of her herd. Clad in a gray work shirt and dark blue jeans, her short brown hair clinging close to her face, she managed to look workmanlike and pretty. A dozen wranglers followed with the herd, only a quarter of the size of the one that moved across the rangeland below. The horses moved pretty much at their own pace, Fargo noted. Darcy had plainly instructed her hands to let them run freely, satisfied the mountain terrain would act to keep them from straying off on their own. He moved the Ovaro forward from the rocks as Darcy drew closer. When she saw him, he watched the surprise sweep through her face. She left the others and rode to where he waited, her brown eyes narrowed at him as she halted.

"Why are you here?" she asked warily.

"A preacher man once told me always help children and damn fools, the first because they need it, the second because they don't know they need it," he said calmly.

"I told you I'm not taking help from anyone screwing her," Darcy said stiffly.

"You won't be. That's history," Fargo said, the answer true enough at the moment. She frowned back as she turned over his words. "I was warned not to help you. Then some unpleasant gents tried to make sure I didn't," he said and her eyes went to the red line at his temple.

"I'm sorry," she said with a rush of concern. "Now, are you satisfied about them, her included?"

"Not completely. There's a lot that needs pinning down," he said. "Like it or not."

She stayed silent as she studied him and then her face relaxed, the feisty pugnaciousness giving way to that sudden little-girl sweetness. "Can't argue with honesty," she said.

"Nothing's changed. I'm here to help you get out of this alive, so's you don't kill yourself doing something that can't be done," he reminded her.

"I settled for that once, guess I can settle for it again," Darcy said with a half shrug. He swung in beside her as she returned to the herd and called out to her hands. "This is Skye Fargo. He'll be breaking trail for us," she said and the men returned nods and waves. Fargo put the Ovaro into a trot as Darcy rode with him and watched him survey the herd.

"Something you don't like?" she asked, reading his face.

"You're already in trouble. You need six more horses carrying extra oats," he muttered.

"I've enough," she said. "I'll bet this slope goes all the way up but levels off into a high plateau. There are high plateaus up here. I've heard prospectors talk of them."

"I'm sure there are and you figure there'll be good grazing grass for your horses," Fargo said.

"Good as any down on the range, maybe better. It's never been grazed over," Darcy said with almost smug confidence. He sighed inwardly but didn't argue with her. She was the kind who had to learn by lessons not words.

"I'll ride ahead and check things out. Keep moving up the slope till I find you again," he said and spurred the horse forward. The slope stayed at a negotiable angle but narrowed, and he grimaced as his eyes swept the high rocks on both sides, the sparse growths of cottonwoods, many twisted and stunted by wind, rain, and unmerciful sun. Nature showed its power to the mountains before it did anywhere else. It had been that way since the dawn of time and would always be so, he thought.

Keeping the horse at a slow, steady pace, he climbed the slope while his eyes swept the surrounding terrain that defined the mountains. No thunderous, sweeping Rockies, no grand, spectacular Tetons, these mountains were made of high rock and deep washes, embracing a jagged wildness that brought a harshness of its own. And their own kind of danger. But it was not just the mountains and its creatures, the wind, and the sun that crept into his awareness. He knew he was no mystic, no shaman in touch with secrets beyond the ken of other men. But he had long ago come to believe in the mysterious ways of forces that were not bound by what we see, hear, touch, or smell. He'd seen those ways at work in the wild creatures and felt their forces within himself, warnings beyond explaining, messages beyond understanding. They were with him again now as he scanned the tall rocks, a danger unknown but not unfelt.

He rode with it and knew that it was real as the slope finally began to level off and Fargo found the end at a high plateau, long and wide and studded with clusters of black oak and hackberry that clung together protectively as though they could defy the fury of the mountain winds. The far edges of the plateau were bordered by high rock formations and Fargo felt his lips draw back in a grimace as he walked the pinto across the grama grass. He halted finally and turned and waited at the top of the slope for Darcy and the herd to arrive. The day was beginning to close down when she came into sight, the mustangs following, spreading out on the plateau as the hands herded them into a loose oval.

He came alongside Darcy as she stared down at the grass, saw the furrow crease her brow, then dismay slide across her face. "It's all dried out, all yellow," she murmured, lifting her eyes to peer across the plateau.

"It'll be the same all over," Fargo said, and her

eyes were uncomprehending as she turned to him. "The grass up here gets the sun first and it dries up first come autumn. Range grass below will last a month longer," he said, and she stared back. "Your horses can't graze on this and you'll be out of oats in days," he added.

"There must be a place where the grass is still green. We just have to find it," she said.

"I wouldn't hold much hope in that," Fargo said.

"I would," she snapped adamantly.

"I'll try come tomorrow," he said as dusk began to descend. "Meanwhile, spread oats and set up your night lines." She dismounted and barked orders to her hands. By the time darkness fell, night lines had been set out to form a loose boundary around the herd as the horses ate the oats that had been put down. Unsaddling the Ovaro, Fargo found Darcy at the far side of the herd, sitting alone on her blanket. She glowered as she met his eyes.

"Don't even think it," she said. "I'm not turning back."

"You might save yourself time and grief," Fargo said.

"I'm sure you'll find a place with good grass up here," she said.

"If I don't?"

"I'll think about that then, not before," she said. He nodded and turned to go. "You can bed down here," she said. "I won't be minding."

"Good enough," he said. He took his bedroll and set it out as Darcy went behind her horse and changed. He was undressed to his shorts when she stepped from behind the horse wearing a short gray cotton nightdress, shapeless in form, yet it allowed a glimpse of firm, sturdy legs, attractive calves, and nicely rounded knees. He saw her take in the muscled beauty of his torso as she folded her legs under her and sat on the blanket and handed him a length of cold beef jerky.

"Trail rations," she said.

"I'm used to that," he said.

"It must be hard," she remarked, and he frowned back. "Trying to help someone you don't believe in," she finished.

He thought for a moment. "Harder for you than me, maybe," he said and watched her turn his answer in her mind.

"I'll have to think on that," she said, finishing her jerky and sliding under the blanket. When he finished, he fitted himself into the bedroll and slept as the night turned cool. He woke first when the morning came, using his canteen to wash, and was half dressed when he saw she was sitting up and watching him. She looked prettier than she'd any right to look just waking up. She said nothing and only watched as he pulled on his shirt and finished dressing.

"Move across the plateau," he said when he had the Ovaro saddled. "I'll come find you." She nodded and he rode away at a trot, setting out over the plateau and its yellowed, lifeless grass. Finally, he turned, veering to the right to ride along one edge of tall rock borders, moving slowly as he peered into the numerous crevices that seemed to thread their way all through the rocks. Once again he felt the uneasiness come to him, prodding and pushing at him with almost mocking glee. He saw a pair of pronghorns with their inwardly curved horns leap effortlessly from rock to rock. A cougar showed itself, caught a glimpse of him, and disappeared. A red fox skittered between crevices to also vanish. But there was more in the mountains, another presence, something that continued to make him uneasy.

His eyes were a brilliant blue in the burning sun as they swept the rock formations, the few twisted trees, the passageways, the sky, and the firm ground of the plateau. Something, he murmured to himself, something. In the distance, he saw the plateau narrowing as it veered westward, the rocks rising up to form a porous wall pierced with passages and draws. But to the far right, he saw a very tall outward curve of sandstone, extending so far that it became a giant, long, deep escarpment. When he rode to it, he saw that its arch was even wider and longer than it had seemed, and when he reached it his eyes scanned the ground. Where the giant escarpment of stone extended, it shut out the burning sun. The grass that grew beneath it was still rich and green.

He continued to stare at the grass as he realized the mixed thoughts that swam through his mind. Should he lead Darcy to the place? The question shimmered. It wouldn't be hard to turn her from it. He could take her to where the plateau curved west, away from the great, arching stone. She'd follow, he knew, and he heard himself cursing softly. Without fresh grass for the herd, the sooner she'd have to turn back. She hadn't enough oats to feed the herd for more than another two days. But the grass under the giant escarpment would provide the herd with enough food to hold them for another three days. He swore again. Three days more for her to continue her futile pursuit. Three days more chance for her to risk real disaster. He would be doing her a favor by steering her away from the escarpment. But he couldn't, dammit, he spit out. She trusted him. He couldn't betray that trust, not even for her own good.

Angrily, he turned the Ovaro, rode back, and came upon Darcy and the herd a little after midday. "This way," he said with a grunt and led her across the plateau to the giant escarpment and the rich grass beneath it. She took a moment to notice the grass and then gave a sharp little cry of delight. "You see, I told you you'd find good grass," she almost squealed. She shouted orders to the hands and moments later the herd was grazing eagerly. "I can save at least two days' worth of oats," Darcy said.

"About that," he said flatly and she tossed him a sharp glance.

"You could sound happier," she said.

"You want a trailsman or an actor?" he said and turned away. "Set up camp here when they're finished grazing. It'll be dark then." He rode from her, made his way through a passage in the high rock formations, and wondered whether he had done the right thing after all. The longer she stayed in the mountains, the more chance there was of real trouble. He rode through the passage, emerged onto a flat ledge of rock that let him scan the distance, and he caught sight of a faraway passage that seemed wide and not too steep. But it was too far away to explore before the day ended and once again he scanned the nearby rocks as the uneasiness returned. He kept feeling they were not alone in these craggy mountains and he rode slowly, his gaze on the ground, seeking prints, signs, anything that would let him read a message. But the ground underfoot was mostly gravel and stone, none of it quick to reveal prints. When the dusk began to encroach on the high rocks, he turned the Ovaro and made his way back down the crags, feeling distinctly on edge.

Everyone had settled down with the night when he reached the escarpment. He set out his bedroll and had finished his own beef strip when Darcy appeared in her short nightgown that gave her a little-girl appearance. "Find a way for us to go in the morning?" she asked.

"Nothing I'm happy with," he grumbled.

"Maybe you're being too choosy," Darcy offered.

He eyed her face, saw her keep it expressionless. "Why would I do that?" he pushed at her.

She spoke slowly, carefully. "You could be too concerned," she said, but there was something left hanging in her voice.

"Or something else?" he said. She let a shrug answer as she strode away. He flung a silent oath after her as he stretched out in the bedroll even as he knew he couldn't wholly blame her. She knew what he thought of her plans. She wasn't aware that his conscience made up for his lack of commitment. But he was, painfully aware, and he went to sleep with a grimace holding his lips. When the new day came, he rose to a sky made of high, wide, towering thunderclouds that were building up in the distance. As he watched, he saw the deep purple of intense storms being generated in the thunderheads. But the sky hung ominously, still undecided which way it would go, its decision made of nature's malicious whims.

Had this been the uneasiness that had been prodding at him, he wondered. He'd seen the restless uneasiness of wild creatures as they picked up impending storms not yet formed. The thought stayed with him as he dressed. He saddled the Ovaro and walked along the edge of the herd, where he found Darcy. She was looking out at the long, narrow gully that cut through the rocks bordered by stone walls on both sides. It cut through the rocks in an almost straight line, as far as the eye could see. "There, that's it," Darcy said excitedly. "It goes east right through the mountain. It'll save us days."

"I'll check out how far it goes," Fargo said.

"It goes plenty far. You can't see the end of it," she said.

"I want to see the end of it," he said.

"We'll be ahead no matter where it ends. That's enough for me," Darcy countered.

"Not for me. You keep to the plateau while I go look," he said.

"The plateau?" she echoed incredulously. "Nonsense, when we have that gully right in front of us. It's practically an avenue. The plateau curves west, entirely out of our way."

"Stay on the plateau," he repeated sternly.

"You know what I'm thinking?" she returned, hands on her hips. "I'm thinking you want to discourage me. You want me to give up. Well, it won't work."

He glared at her. "Keep to the plateau till I get back, dammit," he said and sent the Ovaro into a fast canter. *Damn her suspicious stubbornness,* he muttered to himself as he rode to the rocks. But instead of riding into the gully, he picked his way along the web of narrow crevices and flat ledges that over-looked the gully. He paralleled the deep cut below, saw that it was wide enough for four horses abreast in some places, not more than two in others. Still, it was an inviting pathway as it cut through the high rock formations, but he stayed on the rocky, difficult terrain. As he did, his eyes were more often on the sky than the gully as he watched the thunderclouds grow deeper, higher, and wider.

He rode toward them and felt the muscles of his jaw grow tight. Flashes of lightning pierced the deep purple of the sky that was no longer so distant. The massive thunderheads were moving, still uncertainly, and he watched them with growing alarm. The lightning flashes grew stronger and more frequent. He knew what these tremendous storms could do in the mountains. The rains would come first as the skies seemed to rip open. But not the gentle life-giving rains to nourish the earth and everything on it but a cascade of water assaulting the land below it. The wind would come then, swooping down with demonic fury, churning and driving the rain until there were sheets of water that blotted out all else.

The rain would set upon the mountains as if it had been commanded to fill each niche, cranny, passage, and gully and wash away all and any stones it could dislodge. These storms were the tools that would change the face of the mountains, eroding, filling, smoothing new paths and creating new crags. It would be unceasing in its fury and end as suddenly as it had begun, leaving behind new watering places for man and beast, new moisture for the sun-drenched earth to drink in. Nature often offered a smile after a blow. As he followed the dark, towering clouds, Fargo saw them begin to gather direction and move toward him. As he peered upward, they tore open and in seconds he could see the torrent of rain falling. The storm began to move with frightening speed, the wind suddenly a team of invisible horses pulling the chariot of lightning-filled clouds. The water was already pouring down into the mountain crannies, every passage and gully. In minutes, the gully below him would be filled at the high end under the beginning of the storm.

The water would rise, almost instantly, and begin to roll downward, gaining power and speed with every second in its confined path, bent on sweeping everything before it. But Fargo threaded the horse downward and into the gully, where he immediately put the pinto into an all-out gallop. The wall of water had already started hurtling downward, he knew, but the gully offered the only smooth, direct path to the plateau before being washed to death in the rocks. He had faith in the Ovaro's ability to outrun the cascading wall of water and he sat low in the saddle to cut down wind resistance. It was a race they would have to win or be swept up in a watery fury. The gully's smoothness underfoot was a double-edged sword, letting the Ovaro gallop at full speed but offering an unobstructed funnel for the water.

Only a few minutes passed when he heard the sound he'd hoped not to hear yet, the hissing roar of the cascading water racing down the gully. Seconds later, as the curse fell from his lips, he heard the sound of voices and the hoofbeats of horses. His mouth fell open as he lifted his head and peered down the gully. Shock swept through him first, then fury as the mustangs came into view, the cowhands with them driving the herd up the gully. The horses had their ears back and he saw the whites of their eyes and then he picked out Darcy in the center of the mustangs. "Goddamn, goddamn," he yelled at her as he slowed the pinto. "Go back. Turn. Run like hell. Everybody. Now, goddammit, now." She pulled up as did some of the cowhands as he saw at least fifteen mustangs run past him. He swerved the Ovaro to her, his face livid. "I told you to stay on the plateau," he roared, catching her horse by the cheek strap and yanking it around. "Run, dammit," he shouted as he put the Ovaro into a gallop.

He glanced back and saw the hands starting to turn to follow him and Darcy fall in with them as the hissing roar of the water was suddenly loud. He slowed and let her catch up to him. Looking back up the gully, he could see the wall of water, a dark, racing massive wall of water capped by white spray it tossed up over the rocks on both sides. He saw some of her herd as they tried to turn, run into each other in panic. But the rest of the herd that were behind the leaders had a chance to turn and were now in front, terror giving their legs new strength. They began to streak down the gully, some alongside Darcy and the hands, a few in front. Darcy glanced back as he did and he saw the terror in her face. The onrushing water was gaining on them, hurtling down the gully, driven by its own power now as well as the wind and the torrents of rain that followed. He swore silently and began to wonder if they'd reach the plateau in time.

A glance back showed him that some of the mustangs were already caught up in the rushing wall of water, their bodies picked up and flung about as if they were so many toy horses in a child's bathtub. He brought his eyes back to the gully that seemed to stretch endlessly. Darcy's horse had fallen back a length and he could do nothing about it. There was no time left for anything but survival. He kept racing forward as the hissing roar grew louder, blotting out shouts and the sounds of fleeing horses. He was praying and cursing at the same time when he saw the mouth of the gully come into sight. Flinging a last glance behind, he saw the water rushing at him, engulfing another mustang, a relentless force. Survival was now a matter of seconds and he saw Darcy driving her horse as hard as she could, the rest of the herd and her cowhands racing at her heels.

The water would roll straight out of the gully when it hit the plateau, still a mass of thunderous power. But it would spread out quickly enough, dissipating its power and danger in a matter of minutes over the width of the plateau. "Fall out the minute you hit the plateau, right or left," he shouted back to Darcy, hardly able to hear himself over the terrible hissing roar. He guessed the water was but thirty seconds behind him as he raced out of the gully, swerving the Ovaro to the right at once. He caught a glimpse of Darcy following, then he saw some of the hands. A few swung to the left and the herd, with its own instincts, also fanned out. The roaring ball of water shot from the gully as though it were a cannonball. It stayed together for a half-dozen yards and then, freed of the confining walls and its own momentum, it began to spread out in all directions.

In a kind of almost offhanded capitulation, it

changed from an obliterating, deadly force to harm-lessness and that, too, was the way of the moun-tains. Fargo slowed the Ovaro to a walk as the water continued to pour from the mouth of the gully, slowing some now as the rains lessened. Finally, the rain began to diminish to a scattering of still wind-blown drops. As it came to an end, Fargo saw Darcy sitting alone on her horse. The cowhands were scat-tered about, the remainder of the herd scattered even more, most of them far across the plateau. A tentative shaft of sunlight probed the sky, slanting down at a low angle. The day was not far from an end. Finally, Darcy prodded her horse toward him and he waited, his jaw hard as stone as she came to a halt beside him.

"Congratulations. You get the damn fool award," he threw at her. She stared back, no pugnacious, sassy defiance, only a terrible hollowness as the enormity of what had happened clung to her. "It'll stay with you," he said.

"The storm?"

"Looking death in the face," he said, and her lips tightened as she nodded. She turned as two of the hands rode up.

"How many did we lose?" she asked.

"I'd guess about a quarter of the herd," one of the men said. "I think we can round up the rest by night."

"Do the best you can," she said, and the two men rode away. Darcy's eyes went to Fargo and he saw pain mixed with the shock in her face. "Those poor horses. They run wild in these mountains all the time and nothing happens to them. Why now?" she asked, as much of herself as him.

"They wouldn't have gone into the gully on their own. Instinct, horse sense, call it whatever you like, it would've kept them out. You drove them in," he told her.

"Oh God," she murmured, her hands covering her face. "Oh God."

He pulled her hands down. "It's done. There's no undoing it. You live with it. That's all there's left to do," he said.

She lifted her head and the pugnaciousness came back into her face. "I'll go help round up horses. I'm not turning back," she said. He watched her ride off and decided it was more than stubbornness. She refused to lose. It was her own obsession, perhaps as much a one as Carol's obsession with having her way. He turned and rode alongside the high rocks, still thinking about Darcy, a grudging admiration edging his thoughts. Scanning the land, he was surprised at how quickly the ground drank in the rain. By dusk he found a spot against a buttress of sandstone that was dry enough to spend the night.

Darcy and her hands followed his tracks and appeared with the remainder of her mustangs. Both horses and hands were weary and quick to settle down for the night. Fargo climbed through a crevice in the rocks to where a ledge offered a perfect place to set out his bedroll. He had eaten, undressed, and stretched out when he heard the faint scrape of footsteps. He sat up and Darcy's form appeared, climbing up the crevice toward him. "Watched you come up this way," she said as she lowered herself onto the bedroll, a shawl over the short nightgown. Her eyes roamed across his torso as he sat before her.

"I'm sorry I didn't listen to you," she said, an edge of contrition in her voice.

"That's a start," he commented.

"But I didn't come up just to tell you that," Darcy said.

"What did you come up for?" he asked mildly.

"It's not just what you've done for me," she said.

"You always approach things sideways?" he said.

"I just want you to know that. It's more. It's you," she said, almost a touch of reproach in her voice. "You make a woman want," she added.

"I haven't tried to do that," Fargo said.

"You don't have to try. You just have to be," Darcy said.

"I'm hearing a lot of talk," Fargo pushed at her.

She gave a sudden giggle, lifted her arms, and the shawl and nightdress came off over her head. "Is this better?" she said.

"Much," he said and took in a sturdy body that radiated all the beautiful vigor of youth—strong shoulders, a rounded rib cage, smooth, tight skin. Her breasts echoed the pugnaciousness of her face. He smiled to himself. Not large but very high and very round, they pushed forward with a sassy directness. A tiny pink nipple topped each one, surrounded by an equally small pink areola. As his eyes moved downward, he saw a slightly rounded little belly, a deep indentation in the center, a convex little mound that offered its own surprising sensuousness.

Below, her firm, tight skin curved downward to a neat but puffy little black triangle that was entirely in keeping with the rest of her, a pushy sauciness to it. Her legs were not long and lithe but had a firm, strong smoothness that offered its own attractiveness. He held the opening of the sleeping bag up for her and she almost dived in, turning at once and wrapping herself around him, arms and legs encircling his muscled body. "Oh God, oh, so nice, so nice," she breathed at the touch of skin against skin. His lips found hers and she returned his kiss with warm wetness. He cupped a hand around one of the thrusting direct breasts, felt its vibrant warmth and caressed the tiny tip with his thumb, causing it to rise with a tiny surge of pleasure. Darcy uttered murmured sounds, something between words and moans, a kind of soft purring. "Jeez, oh Jeez . . . yes, yes, aaaah, yes," she said, finding words as he drew the high, round breast into his mouth, pulling gently and rolling his tongue around the tiny tip.

Her hands dug into his back and her firm, compact body twisted, lifted, and fell back as his hands moved downward. He smoothed his way across the convex little belly and down further to the small triangle. His fingers slid through the dense nap. It was surprisingly soft, with none of the usual filamentous touch to it, but a byssus feel, pleasant and inviting. He lingered, pressing down on the Venus mound beneath. Darcy groaned. "Yes, yes . . . go on, go on," she breathed and he felt her fingers close around his wrist and press his hand downward. "Please, please . . . yes, oh yes," she murmured and followed with a choking gasp of delight as he touched the wet satiny lips and felt her inner thighs moist with the sweet ambrosia of desire.

Darcy's hips surged upward as he explored further, sliding his fingers along the dark, moist walls of silk. Her moans grew louder and her hand reached for him again, groping, and finally finding him. She gave a sharp cry of pure pleasure. She held his throbbing warmth for a moment and then pulled him to her, pushing her hips forward. Her thighs were hanging open, trembling with wanting. "Yes, yes, oh Jeez . . . aaaah, aaaah, yes," Darcy moaned, lifting her hips for him, the unvarnished pleading of the senses. Only when he came to her, letting himself touch her and then slide forward, did she pull her hand away, uttering a deep, groaning cry. He felt the strength of her smooth, muscled legs as they clasped around him. She pulled his head down to push one thrusting breast into his mouth, crying out as she began to move with him, matching his slow thrustings first, then moving faster, leading in a sinuous, horizontal dance.

She clung as she rose and fell with him and she made little joyful sounds. It was plain that Darcy more than enjoyed the pleasures of eros. She reveled in the moment, carrying enjoyment to another height, carrying every part of her into pleasure, every part of her pleading, demanding, taking, giving. Making love was no passion limited to the organs of sex but involved her entire body, arms, hands, legs, belly, breasts, knees, and face as she rubbed and writhed and slid and pressed herself to him. Her contagion transferred itself to him and he found new pleasures in her complete surrender to touch, taste, sight, and sound. "More, oh more," Darcy murmured as he moved in her, slowly, then faster, slowing again, increasing the rhythm once more, and before he heard her quick gasps he felt the soft contractions of her, embraces of ecstasy as never-changing and primeval as the beginning of mankind.

"Yeeeeeesss," Darcy screamed, a sudden outburst, an affirmation of pleasure, and her strong legs clamped even tighter around him. She stiffened, trembled, and stiffened again, rising up and finally falling back. A long, groaning sigh escaped her and she lay still, hardly breathing. It was a while before her legs relaxed and fell from him. She half turned, eyes closed, and pushed one high, firm breast against his face. The senses still demanded touch, unwilling to let go of pleasure. He held her and felt her body relax and finally heard the soft, steady breathing as she fell asleep. He closed his eyes and slept with her until morning came. Waking, he looked at her as she lay against him, her sturdy body and high, direct breasts giving her a special loveliness, as if even asleep she radiated energy. He slid from the bedroll, washed, and dressed quickly in the cool of the morning and she was sitting up when he finished. A Cheshire cat smile edged her lips. "I hope she's really history, now," Darcy murmured.

He shook his head in wonderment. "That's what stays with you?" he asked.

"That's what stays with every woman," she said.

"I'll remember that," he said. History was yesterday, he could have told her, not necessarily tomorrow. But he said nothing and she rose and pulled on the nightdress and shawl and hurried down the crevice to where she had her things. He strolled down soon after her and saddled the Ovaro. He had just finished when Darcy came up to him. "The plateau narrows as it curves west. Stay on it till I find a better way," he said.

She nodded and read the question in his eyes. "Promise," she said. He grunted and swung into the saddle. She'd hold to it, he was certain. Yesterday was too fresh in her mind to push aside.

6

Fargo rode into the high rocks where the crags stared down at him from their newly washed heights like so many frowning sentinels. Yesterday's furious storm was gone but not without leaving reminders. Some of the great stone formations hadn't dried and huge water marks still stained their uneven façades. Little rivulets of water still trickled their way down narrow apertures and stone basins held small pools of fresh water. Pieces of broken tree branches were scattered throughout the rocks. He expected those things. What he hadn't expected was the uneasiness that returned to wrap itself around him again. He frowned at it and felt it set his body tingling.

One thing became instantly clear. He had misread its veiled message. He had thought the impending storm had sent the signals. But he'd been wrong. The storm was gone and there was still danger hovering near. The inner voice that continued to push at him was all the proof he needed and automatically his eyes swept the surrounding rocks. But he saw nothing and swore softly as he sent the Ovaro across a flat ledge and down a succession of narrow passages. Below, the plateau was narrowing and he saw a wall of sandstone rising in the distance to end its path. As he continued to probe the craggy hills he came on a wide path that led to a long draw bordered by high rock on one side and a lower wall on the other. It ran east, further than he could see, and it offered the only path through the craggy maze. A quick glance at the sky showed it was a cloudless, clear blue. He sent the pinto downward and rode back to where he met Darcy coming along the plateau.

"Follow me," he said, and she motioned to the hands, who brought the herd up after her. It was late afternoon when he reached the wide path that led into the draw. "It goes east. Stay on it," he told Darcy. "I'll meet you later." His eyes lifted, sweeping the top of the high wall at one side of the draw.

"What is it?" Darcy asked.

"Nothing. Just checking," he said and silently swore at the disquiet that stayed with him. Turning from her, he sent the Ovaro up a narrow passage, then another and another after that, until he finally reached the top of the high wall. A level ledge ran along the top of the wall and he peered down at the plateau and Darcy as he rode along the top of the high rocks. Again, he scanned the crags and passages and once again had only the uneasiness clinging to him. The rock underfooting and small gravel patches made picking up prints almost impossible and he swore in frustration as he rode, slowly investigating every niche he found as he continued to sweep the high rocks with long, probing glances.

But the gray-purple of dusk began to slip over the high land and he threaded his way downward until he reached the plateau below. The night had almost settled in when he met Darcy and waved her to the side of the draw against the high wall. "Bed down here," he said, unsaddling the pinto.

"Guess it's lucky I'm exhausted," Darcy said, and he questioned with a glance. "There's no place to get away alone," she said.

"Tomorrow night," he said and finished setting out his things. After a meal of cold beef jerky, he lay down in the sleeping bag and Darcy came to wrap herself in her blanket alongside him. He listened to her restlessly twist and turn. "Thought you were exhausted," he said.

"Maybe I'm too tired," she answered.

"Thought maybe you might be having second thoughts," he said.

"No," she snapped at once. "Losers have second thoughts. That's why they lose."

She settled down at once and he gave her credit for the kind of absolute determination that refused to allow a negative thought. Perhaps sheer willpower did make things happen, he mused as sleep came to him and the night stayed silent. He rose first with the morning, washed and dressed and peered along the length of the draw. "Keep on it," he told Darcy when she woke and dressed. "I'll be checking back later." He saddled the Ovaro and again climbed through narrow crevices until he reached the top of the high wall. The sun was already burning, baking the rocks, and he peered down to where Darcy and the herd were a parade of small figures moving down the draw close to the high wall.

He returned his attention to the high rocks as he made his way along the flat top of the wall, pausing to peer into every niche and crevice. When the sun told him the day had reached noon, he halted, dismounted, and drank from his canteen, then let the Ovaro do the same. He shaded his eyes to squint into the distance. The draw continued to stretch onward. He wondered if he dared hope that it might stretch though most of the mountain. Perhaps Darcy's confidence would be rewarded after all. He would have been able to relax except for the damn unease that clung to him, and once again he searched the high rocks, letting his eyes move up, down, and along each towering formation. He had just swung back into the saddle when it happened, a burst of brilliance, a split-second flash of light, so fast he had no chance to pinpoint it before it was gone. But it had come from somewhere in the rocks ahead.

Frowning, he leaned in the saddle to peer down to the draw below. Because he had been moving so slowly and carefully, Darcy and the herd were out of sight somewhere up ahead. He returned his eyes to the crags and rocks as he sent the pinto forward. Only a few minutes passed when it came again, another flash of light, gone as quickly as it had come. But he'd caught the fleeting burst of it, the sun glinting on something, reflecting for an instant flash. A mirror, he wondered. Or something metal, a belt buckle, a prospector's pan, something. Fargo moved the Ovaro forward again, his eyes sweeping the mountain. A few minutes passed when the flash came again, but this time he glimpsed enough to pinpoint the location. It had come from further on along the high wall where he rode and he pushed the Ovaro as fast as he dared. Another flash came and vanished and Fargo veered from the flat ledge to move along behind a line of low rocks that let him make better time.

His eyes swept the distant ledge when he suddenly

heard the sharp sound. Taking a moment to listen, he recognized the impact of rock being pounded. He reined to a halt, swung to the ground, and pulled the rifle from its saddle case. Staying behind the rocks as he ran forward on silent steps, he saw the figures come into sight—four men all at the very edge of the wall of high rock. Three of them were using pickaxes to open small holes in the rock and as he watched, another flash of light came as the sun caught the flat side of a pickax. Prospectors, he thought, the first thought that came to him. But he discarded it immediately and a frown furrowed his brow. No prospectors. This was no rock for prospecting. Never. He crept closer and saw the fourth man inserting what looked like small stakes into the holes made in the rock. But again he instantly corrected himself. No stakes. The man was inserting sticks of dynamite, the fuses now visible hanging from each.

Jesus, he swore as a sense of helplessness and rage swept through him. He brought up the rifle, took aim, and fired. The nearest of the four figures spun as he fell. The other three dropped, yanking out their guns; one put a match to the fuse of one of the dynamite sticks. He flung oaths at them as they dived, rolled, and raced away, staying low as they ran. He fired again and one of them went sprawling and lay still. Fargo started to run toward the dynamite sticks but skidded to a halt as he saw the fuse was almost at an end. He spun, half ran and half dived behind a tall stone a dozen feet back from the edge of the high rocks. He landed behind it and curled himself up in a little ball tight against the thick slab of stone just as the first stick of dynamite exploded.

The roar filled the mountaintop. Three more explosions followed instantly as the first one set off the others. Through the roar he heard the sounds of rocks exploding apart, slamming into each other, arching upward, then cascading down into the gully below. They'd reach the bottom in seconds, smashing, crashing, destroying. Darcy and the herd would be there. They had watched, waited, and planned it, timing the attack. Fargo cursed in helplessness as a lone rock, flung off by itself, smashed into the big stone formation he hid behind. Finally, the crashing roar began to die away, only the clatter of smaller stones remaining. He stepped away from his protective stone mantle and didn't bother to look over the side, unwilling to see what he knew he'd find below. He ran to where he'd left the Ovaro, pulled himself onto the horse, and began to pick his way downward through the network of narrow passages.

When he emerged into the gully he turned to where the mass of fallen rock lay strewn across the ground, reaching almost to the other side of the passage. Dismounting, he made his way on foot, skirting fallen rocks, climbing over some. His lips drew back in distaste as he passed the broken bodies of horses, some still pitifully clinging to life, others already smashed into death. He cursed those who had done this, their greed and their ruthlessness, but mostly their callous disregard for life. If Carol was a part of it she'd pay, he muttered. But that was still very much an open question, he reminded himself. He cursed softly as he passed a boulder with the bodies of two of Darcy's men underneath it, and he tried to close his ears to the terrible whinny of a horse in pain. He continued to search through the mass of rocks and he was nearing the end of them when he saw Darcy.

Shaking, she stood with her back pressed against the far wall, her horse alongside her. She fell into his arms when he reached her, long sobs wracking her body. "I tried to stop them. I was too late," he said.

"I heard the shots. I was looking up when the rocks exploded. That's the only reason I'm alive. I had a few extra seconds to get over here," Darcy said. "I'll never forget those rocks falling at me, never." He heard a voice, then another, and turned to see two of Darcy's hands climbing over rocks toward them, both wearing smeared bloodstains on their heads. "You the only two that made it?" Darcy asked, and both men nodded, their faces drained. Fargo turned to Darcy and put his hands on her shoulders.

"There's nothing left here," he said firmly yet gently. "It's time to go back. You can't go on."

She stared back for a long moment and the pain darkened her eyes. "There's no reason now," she agreed, her voice a monotone. She turned to the two hands. "You two come with me. I'm not leaving these horses to die in misery." Fargo stayed as the two men followed her, and in moments the shots echoed through the gully as Darcy made her way through the fallen rocks. It took a while, each shot deliberate and accurate. Mercy was sometimes made of pain, he reflected unhappily. All too often.

When she returned she didn't look at him and her cheeks were glistening with wet stains. It was only after he led the way down the mountain passage that she spoke, coming alongside him. "You satisfied now?" she pushed at him, reproach in her voice. "She had to know."

"That's still a maybe," he said.

"Not to me," Darcy flung back. "I want them dead, for what they did, all of them."

"The ones behind it will pay, believe me," Fargo said.

"Her, too?"

"If she was part of it," Fargo said.

"You said she was history. I think you're still soft on her," Darcy accused.

"It's nothing to do with Carol," Fargo said. "It's to do with me. I have to be sure. I want to be able to sleep when it's finished."

She fell silent but he knew she hadn't really accepted his answer. He couldn't blame her. She had her certainties. This had only reinforced them. Reason always ran a poor second to emotions. He found a spot to bed down as darkness fell and watched Darcy curl up on her blanket. He let her embrace aloneness. Besides the hurting, there was anger inside her and that was good. It gave her something to cling to besides the pain. He stretched out and let sleep come to him and heard her sob during the night. She woke red-eyed with the morning and, already dressed, he watched her douse her face with cold water. He felt her eyes on him after she'd dressed, watching him saddle the Ovaro. "You mean what you said, about making them pay?" she asked.

"Count on it," he said and she grunted, an acceptance still not complete. He smiled to himself, willing to settle for that. She rode with him, the two hands staying back as he led the rest of the way out of the mountains. Fargo knew they had cut traveling time going through the mountains, even with all the setbacks, and when they reached the range he was not surprised to see the dark mess of horses in the distance.

"Bastards. Murderers," Darcy hissed. Fargo peered out to where the combined herds moved, their range riders hard to pick out but plainly keeping the large mass of horses in line.

"Let's get back," he said. "There's nothing to be done here." He began to pull the pinto around when he pulled the horse to a halt as he saw the line of near-naked riders coming out of a stand of cottonwoods some thousand yards ahead. Their eyes were on the big herd of horses and he squinted to pick out the few markings on their pony blankets. "Pawnees," he said, taking in the triangular decorations and the silver armbands the Pawnee favored. He watched the Indians move toward the herd from behind. They soon began to speed up their pace. "They're going to attack," Fargo muttered.

"They'll raid the herd. They do it all the time, swoop down, cut out a dozen or so horses and make off with them," Darcy said. "They've done it to me. Nobody tries too hard to stop them and provoke an all-out fight. The Pawnee are satisfied to run off with a dozen horses. I think it's like counting coup with them, and showing they can do whatever they want."

"And the wranglers just move on with the rest of the herd," Fargo said, and Darcy nodded. "Maybe not this time," Fargo said as thought gathered inside him.

"Meaning what?" Darcy frowned.

"They'd have no herd at all if the Pawnee drove them all off," Fargo said.

"They're satisfied with the raids. Why would they go all out?" Darcy questioned.

"If they had the right reasons," he said.

"You're talking in riddles," she said.

"I've an idea. If I can make it work, Dave Cord and the others won't have any horses to sell," he said.

"Is that a big if or a little if?" Darcy questioned.

"A big if," he admitted. "You get out of here, go home, take your boys with you."

"When will you come back?"

He thought for a moment. "A day, maybe two," he said. "Now go." She rode away, her face tight, the two hands following, and he waited till she vanished from sight behind a stand of hackberry. Bringing his eyes back to the distance, he spurred the Ovaro forward, closer to where the Pawnee was now almost full-out. He halted behind a small cluster of black oak and let his plans form themselves. They excited him even as he knew they might not get off the ground. But they were worth the try. Cord and the others deserved to have their herds driven off. It'd be a kind of down payment, Fargo pondered. The rest would follow when he had the proof he wanted. Carol swam into his thoughts. He'd have to return for her. He was still not making assumptions.

Sending the pinto forward, he moved to a closer cluster of oak, his eyes fastened on the Pawnee as they suddenly went into a full gallop. They charged, knifing into one corner of the herd with expert ease. A dozen of the Indians set up a covering barrage of arrows and gunfire while the others separated the dozen horses from the rest of the herd. Darcy had been right. The wranglers set up a return fire but it was a weak effort, aimed more at keeping the rest of the herd in place than the Pawnee. As the Indians raced off with their horses they sent whoops of glee across the range and Fargo stayed in the trees and watched them race away.

He turned his eyes on the herd and caught a glimpse of Carol's sandy hair as she rode hatless, turning back a horse trying to wander off alone. She melted in with the herd as it moved on and Fargo stayed in the trees until the mass of horses were no longer in sight. Slowly, he moved into the open and picked up the trail of prints left by the Pawnee. They had turned their captured horses north across the range, he saw, over a half-dozen shallow hills and through a wide but loose forest of red cedar. He followed, not hurrying, and the afternoon was drawing to an end when he neared their camp inside the oak. He smelled the woodsmoke first, then heard the sounds of voices and horses. He kept the Ovaro at a walk, pushing through the scaly branches. There were no sentries. The Pawnee felt secure and with reason, he saw as he moved to the outer parameters of the camp.

It was a full-size home camp with at least twenty teepees, a long smokehouse, a stream running through the center, their horses tethered to ropes at the rear of the camp. He glimpsed naked children, bare-breasted squaws, and loin-clothed bucks moving inside the camp and at least two cookfires, hide and meat-drying racks and boiling pits. He kept the Ovaro at a steady, slow walk as he reached the outer edge of the camp. The Pawnee spoke the Caddoan language, along with the Arikara and the Wichita. It wasn't a tongue he knew well, but it was related to the Siouan which he did know and most Pawnee could understand Siouan. A middle-aged squaw saw him first, and she let out a short scream. Others spun at once and after the initial shouts of alarm and surprise, a hush fell over the camp as he moved forward. Two big bucks ran forward, seized the cheek strap of the Ovaro, and led him between the widely spaced rows of teepees, halting before the last and largest one.

A figure stepped from the teepee, plainly the chief, an eagle feather in his braided black hair, silver armbands around his biceps, a silver pendant hanging from around his neck. But it was his mien that marked him at once, his eyes black and hard as onyx, his bearing imperious, commanding, a tall man with the typically massive, heavy face of the Pawnee. "Hear me, chief of the Pawnee," Fargo said in Siouan. "I come to give and to take," he said and using a sign language, he made the gesture of an exchange. The chief motioned to a slender figure standing with the others who had quickly crowded around and spoke to him in Caddoan. The brave addressed Fargo in a mixture of Siouan and English.

"The chief of the Pawnee listens," he said, and Fargo dismounted, aware it would be considered disrespectful to converse with a chief while looking down from horseback.

"The few horses mean nothing. It is the others that will make the Pawnee sorry," Fargo said, and the slender figure translated. "They are going to the bluecoat pony soldiers, who will ride them to attack the Pawnee." He halted, saw the chief's eyes widen and then narrow at him.

"Why do you come to tell this?" the chief asked.

Again, Fargo used sign language to supplement his words, making the gesture of being expelled and being angry. "My answer. The Pawnee can give me revenge," he said. "And the Pawnee can strike a real coup. Exchange," he said, again using the sign language for the word.

He caught the glimmer of contempt across the Pawnee chief's face, but he also saw anticipation form in the black eyes. He held the sigh of relief inside himself. It had worked. But his moment was shattered as the chief barked orders and four of the braves seized him, one yanking the Colt from his holster. "I came in honor. I expected the same from the Pawnee," Fargo protested.

"The chief thinks you do not know much about honor," the slender brave translated. "You know only about revenge. But the Pawnee are not without honor. After we strike, you will be free to go."

"Why does the chief wait for that?" Fargo questioned.

"To be sure there are no tricks," the man said, and Fargo was marched to a stake in the ground near one of the teepees. Rawhide thongs tied his ankles to the stake and his wrists were bound together in front of him. The bonds gave him enough slack to sit or kneel but not stand. His gunbelt was taken and the chief carried it and the Colt into his teepee, Fargo noted as he sat on the ground. He became an instant object of curiosity for the camp children and some of the squaws while the Pawnee chief retired to his teepee with a half dozen of his braves.

Fargo stayed quietly as some of the children poked and prodded at him. He swore at the unexpected turn of things but knew it could have been worse. They hadn't searched him beyond the gun and holster. The double-edged throwing knife was still in the narrow holster around his calf. It would have to stay there till the night was still. He forced himself to relax and watched the squaws build up both fires for the night. But instead of the camp sliding into sleep, Fargo watched it grow suddenly more active. Frowning, he saw braves and squaws emerging from teepees and beginning to gather around the fire furthest from where he sat at the stake. Next they began to bring out war drums, tom-toms, and the larger log drums.

Fargo cursed softly even before the chief appeared; he walked to the fire and sat down cross-legged before it. The dancers appeared next, costumed in feathers, headdresses, and war paint. Fargo swore silently again. The chief had plainly decided there wouldn't simply be a raid to scatter the herd. It had suddenly taken on more importance. There'd be an all-out attack as well, and Fargo's lips pulled back in a grimace. The need to get to Carol before the attack had taken on new, grim proportions, but his chance to do so had suddenly shrunk. He had counted on the time while the camp slept to cut himself free and that time had all but disappeared. The war dances would go on through most of the night, and the Pawnee would be up and awake and all over the camp. As if in confirmation, a bare-chested brave folded himself on the ground a few feet from where Fargo stayed tied to the stake. Moments later, two squaws sat down a few feet away on the other side of him and Fargo groaned in frustration.

He sat and helplessly watched as the dancers went on and the hours dragged by. He cursed again as the moon passed the midnight hour, hanging high in the sky for a long moment before traveling slowly on its downward path. He tried bringing his bound hands down to his trouser leg and the two squaws looked at him immediately. He stretched his arms and sat back and silently cursed. The dancing and drumming continued until the night began edging toward a close. Finally, the chief rose and went to his teepee, and the ceremonies came to an end. Some of the braves went into teepees, but most fell down and lay on the ground. They rested but they were too keyed up to sleep, Fargo knew, and he waited as the two squaws near him rose and left. The brave did the same soon after, and Fargo scanned the length of the camp, pausing at each cluster of prostrate figures.

Once more, he reached his bound wrists down to the edge of his trouser leg, curled the tips of his fingers under the material, and lifted until he could feel the smooth leather of the calf holster. He reached the hilt of the thin blade, got a precarious grasp on it, and pulled it free. Turning the knife in his fingers, he managed to grasp it securely enough to be able to push and pull the sharp edges against the rawhide. Slowly, he began to saw the thongs, but the awkwardness of his position allowed him only short, maddeningly slow cuts. The rawhide was sinewy and tough and his fingers cramped up every few minutes. Over and over, he had to stop and give his hands time to uncramp before going on. Little beads of perspiration formed across his forehead as he doggedly sawed at the thongs. They came not from the physical efforts so much as the knowledge that time was running out on him. And on Carol.

He was sawing at the thongs after he'd stopped to rest when he saw the first streak of dawn spear its way across the sky. He cursed, pulling at the thongs with all his strength. But they still held and he returned to cutting again. The streak of dawn widened. "No, no, not yet," he heard himself hiss. His plan and saving Carol pretty much depended on his being free and reaching the herd before the Pawnee descended. Now he saw his plan shredding before his eyes. The dawn's pink-gray light continued to spread and he saw the night seem to roll up onto itself as it fled. Figures began to rise, stand, and stretch, and then move about. As he continued to saw his short strokes against the rawhide he saw the Pawnee begin to collect bows, arrows, rifles, and tomahawks. Others rose and did the same and the entire camp was quickly awake.

The time was at hand and Fargo felt the bitterness well up inside him. As over a dozen Pawnee came toward him on their way to where the horses were tethered, he quickly pushed the thin blade up into his shirtsleeve, pressed his arm against his ribs and held the blade in place. Each cast a glance his way and he kept his face sullen, which was no problem for him. Helpless fury churned inside him as he saw the chief come from his teepee and join his braves. In but a few minutes, the Pawnee rode from the camp behind their chief and Fargo was struck by their silence. No shouts, no war whoops, no talking, only the soft sound of unshod pony hooves. He watched till they disappeared in the cedar and brought his glance back to the camp. Squaws, children, and old men were the only ones left and Fargo dropped the blade down from his shirtsleeve and began to saw at the thongs again, new desperation giving him new strength.

He had never been so unhappy to see the sun come up and he forced his cramped fingers to stay at their task. He was sawing hard when the knife suddenly dropped from his grip and hit the ground. He cursed when he realized his wrists had come apart, the thongs parted. Flexing his fingers for a moment to let blood course back through them, he scooped up the knife and restored it to the calf holster. His first stop had to be at the chief's teepee to get his Colt and his gaze moved across the women and the old men that were beginning chores for the day. Slowly, he pushed to his feet and began to stroll toward the teepee, moving slowly, trying to stay unnoticed. He was halfway to the teepee when he heard the shouts, surprise at first, then alarm. Fargo dug his heels into the ground and began to run hard. When he reached the teepee, he raced inside to see the Colt and gunbelt hanging from a pole.

He pulled them down, strapped on the gunbelt, and stepped from the teepee. He stopped at once, when he found himself facing a half circle of squaws, old men, and some older children. The women held spears, the old men bows with arrows on their bowstrings, and the older children clubs and tomahawks. His eyes traveled across their faces and he saw no fear in any of them, only hate and grim determination. At first they seemed an almost laughable collection, but as he stared back he realized they were not that at all. In their faces he saw no quarter, no retreat, no fear. He could probably shoot his way through them, he pondered, but he grimaced at the idea of shooting down women and children. Yet perhaps there was no other way, he realized. They were prepared to kill him with a mass attack.

Could he shoot his way out, he found himself wondering. Or was he certain to take more than one spear, more than one arrow? He pushed aside further thoughts as they began to move toward him, tightening the half circle. He moved backward toward the teepee and they closed in after him, their steps a soft, shuffling sound. One thing had become clear. There could be no impasse, no standoff. He couldn't afford one, they wouldn't permit one. They kept shuffling toward him and he moved back again, his thoughts racing. He needed a surprise, something to give him a chance to run. When he felt his back touch the teepee, he whirled and dashed into the tent as an arrow hurtled into the edge of the entrance flap.

Inside, his eyes darted around the teepee, halting at the three sticks that burned in a stone pit to give light to the interior. The thought exploding inside him, he seized one of the sticks, pulled it up, and the one end instantly flared up more brightly. Holding the flame to the bottom of the teepee, he saw the dry, old hides catch fire at once and put the burning stick to another section of the teepee. The flames leaped quickly up along the hides, spreading as heavy smoke from the old hides accompanied the fire. The smoke hole at the top of the teepee did the rest, pulling the air inside up, creating a draft, and in moments the teepee was a pyramid of fire and thick smoke. Fargo wrapped his kerchief around his mouth and dropped low to the ground as the flames and smoke shot from the smoke hole. It seemed only seconds before the fire turned the hides into flaming curls and as the teepee began to collapse, the thick smoke spread outward.

He heard the shouts and screams from outside as, using the smoke as a shield, he raced from what had been the teepee. The Colt in hand, he fired, blindly and wildly, and heard the figures dive for cover as they shouted. The smoke stayed with him longer than he'd hoped it, but finally he emerged and quickly got his bearings and raced for where the Ovaro was tethered with a few remaining ponies. Screams were following him now, but a quick glance back showed him that the women were still disorganized. He was at the Ovaro, vaulting into the saddle when the squaws began to come after him. He left them shouting oaths at him as he sent the horse racing through the cedar.

He rode hard as he cursed. The Pawnee had a good start on him, perhaps too good. None of it had gone the way he planned. Was it beyond salvaging? He rode with his lips drawn back in a grimace, afraid to think about the answer.

ered with a few remaining ponies. Some ans were fol
lowing them. But none of it could stop him.

thatthe
breast.
rode wit

7

Their prints showed that the Pawnee stayed in the cedar after they reached the rangeland, moving along in the tree cover until they neared the herd. Fargo veered when he saw the Pawnee stay in the cedar, unwilling to move any closer and risk being discovered. He turned off and struck out across the relatively open rangeland to come up on the other side. He had turned again and sent the pinto east when he heard the shots and the wild war whoops. The herd came into view and Fargo cursed as he saw it was under full attack, pressed against a wall of cottonwoods at one side by the Pawnee. He kept the Ovaro at a full gallop as he saw the Indian warriors were sending the herd scattering in all directions. He turned into the cottonwoods as he drew closer to the wild scene of racing horses and shouting riders.

He peered forward, trying to find Carol and the others amid the crush of galloping Pawnee and fleeing mustangs. The ground was already littered with lifeless figures, the herd riders who had been the first targets of the Pawnee attack. The Indians were driving off the herd with speed and efficiency, he saw, and the fury of their initial attack had already lessened. He slowed inside the cottonwoods, and squinting at the Pawnee who rode back and forth in wild exuberation, he suddenly caught the glint of sandy hair in the sunlight. He pulled to a halt and saw Carol, a prisoner between the chief and another Pawnee. They rode away from most of the other war-whooping braves and started back across the range with her as the others gradually fell into line behind the chief and his captive.

"Damn," Fargo swore as he watched from the trees. The Pawnee were returning to their camp, where the chief wouldn't be happy at what he found. Fargo's lips were drawn tight. He'd have to pay another visit to the Pawnee camp, even though it might be doomed to fail. He had no choice. He had set wheels in motion that had taken a spin he hadn't expected and Carol was paying the price. He couldn't sit back and let that happen, whether she was part of the attacks on Darcy or not. But there was time enough for another visit to the Pawnee camp. Meanwhile, he stayed in the cottonwoods until the last of the Pawnee were beyond sight. Slowly, he moved the Ovaro from the trees and walked the horse amid the bodies that lay on the ground. He only recognized one and he paused by it for a moment, staring down at Ed Buckley, who lay with four arrows in him.

The others had managed to get away, Dave Cord, Amos Stockel, Marty Schotter. None had stayed to try and save Carol, he noted in disgust. Did that say something, he wondered. Did it show that Carol wasn't that close to them? Or had it just been every man for himself, the ultimate pull of self-preservation? He grunted and cast aside further attempts to find meanings where there probably were none and turned the Ovaro and rode across the range until he reached the long stand of red cedar and pushed into the forest. He held the pinto at a trot, but it was still well into the afternoon when he reached the Pawnee camp. The Indians hadn't arrived much before him, their excited shouts and general bustle proof of that. Plenty of day still clung to the land. He dismounted and tied the Ovaro to a low branch, going forward on foot.

Soon he lowered himself to a crouch and then flattened himself onto his stomach to crawl forward. A dense thicket of tall ironweed, with its thick stems and purplish flowers, closed around him, shielding him as he crawled closer to the camp. He allowed himself a moment of grim satisfaction as he took in the charred remains of the chief's teepee. Shifting his gaze, he quickly found the chief standing before Carol, who was flanked by two braves. "He has escaped and left a curse behind him," Fargo heard the chief say to Carol. "But no matter. The bluecoat soldiers will have no new horses to ride against the Pawnee."

"What are you talking about?" Carol frowned as one of the braves translated for her in halting English.

"The horses you were bringing to the bluecoat soldiers," the chief said.

"We weren't bringing them to any soldiers," Carol said, her frown deepening.

The chief's motion was quick as he slapped her across the face. "Do not lie. He told us," the Pawnee said.

"Who?" Carol questioned, rubbing her hand across her cheek.

"The one who came here, the one on the pinto the color of black rock and snow," the chief said. Fargo saw Carol's eyes widen as she stared at the Pawnee chief.

"Fargo," Carol breathed. "Son of a bitch."

The chief reached out, yanked Carol's shirt open and let his eyes take in the longish breasts that swayed ever so gently as she drew in a deep breath. "It has been a long night and a long day. I will save you for tomorrow," the Pawnee said, nodding his head toward two braves, who seized Carol and marched her away. Fargo saw them take her into a teepee with a yellow, round sun painted on one side. He watched and when the two braves emerged, they were alone. He stayed in the iron-weeds, watching as several squaws entered the teepee. As dusk began to drop over the camp, a young buck took up guard outside, a tomahawk in the waistband of his breechcloth. Fargo kept watch as dusk turned to night and cookfires were lighted in the camp. The chief took up quarters in one of the other teepees with two guards outside, and Fargo didn't try to move until the cookfires burned out and the camp settled down to sleep. He pushed himself from the ground then, carefully moving forward but circling the edges of the camp.

He slowed when he reached the area where the Pawnee had their ponies. The moonlight was rising when he finally found Carol's horse standing a head over the short-legged Indian ponies. He crept forward to the horse and untied the knot that bound the reins to the long rope tether of the other horses.

Moving very slowly, he led Carol's horse to a place in the ceders at the rear of the camp and wrapped the reins around a low branch and went on alone. He reached the rear of the camp and crept sideways until he was behind the teepee with the yellow sun painted on it. Drawing the narrow blade from its calf holster, he pushed it into his belt, where he could reach it in a split-second, and knelt at the edge of the teepee. His eyes searched for a hole, a tear, something that would let him peer inside. But there was none, and he swore silently.

If he cut a hole in the teepee and Carol was alone inside, he would have her free in seconds. If she was not alone, it would be over for both of them. The alarm would be instant, the response even quicker. He stared at the tall tent that was suddenly a puzzle box, defying, taunting, daring him to risk everything. He was tempted. He'd take the dare if it were just him. But he wasn't alone. He had put Carol here. He'd come to make amends for that, not do it again. He slid his feet silently along the rear of the teepee until he was at the side. Then he slid forward again and dropped to one knee. The brave was there, standing sentry, his back to the entrance flap. Fargo's eyes went out to sweep the camp. It was dark and still but he saw a number of sleeping figures dotting the ground. His eyes went back to the sentry. The man was standing, but Fargo saw his shoulders twitch as he swayed, catching himself, fighting to stay awake.

Fargo slid forward and stayed close to the side of the teepee. He thought of using the throwing knife and his hand closed around the hilt, but he pulled it away. If he threw the knife, the sentry would fall be-

121

fore he could reach him. His fall could be loud enough to wake one of the sleeping figures. Moving on the balls of his feet, darting forward when he was close, Fargo brought one arm around the sentry's throat and tightened it at once. The Pawnee came awake and tried to turn and shout, but the arm around his neck had already closed the air from his windpipe. He went limp and Fargo lowered him to the ground, spinning to go into the teepee and halting. The presence of the sentry didn't necessarily mean Carol was alone inside.

He carefully lifted the flap and peered inside. A small fire in a hollow rock afforded a dim light in the teepee. Carol sat with ankles and wrists bound. Her eyes were closed, he saw, and close to her an old squaw sat cross-legged, her eyes very open. He had only one course open to him and it depended on speed. Almost diving, he burst into the teepee. He managed to get at the old squaw just as she opened her mouth to scream. His short, chopping right to her jaw ended the scream before it began and she toppled onto her side. He saw Carol's eyes snap open and clapped one hand to her mouth. "Don't talk. Don't make a sound," he hissed. "Just do what I tell you to do." She nodded and he drew his hand from her mouth, pulled out the knife, and cut her wrist bonds, then her ankle thongs. He pulled her to her feet and started to turn when he heard the sound from outside the teepee. Motioning her to stay in place, he stepped to the flap of the teepee and pulled back the edge of it. "Goddamn," he swore, his lips barely moving. The chief and at least a dozen braves were outside the teepee, with another dozen hurrying over.

It was all suddenly clear. The sentry had not simply been a sentry. He had also been a decoy. At least some of the sleeping figures had been watching him. The Pawnee chief had suspected someone would come for Carol. Spinning on his heel, Fargo stepped to the back of the teepee, raised the knife, and sliced a long cut in the hide, long enough for him to push Carol through. He followed her out, knowing he had perhaps another forty-five seconds. They'd rush the teepee by then, he was certain. He ran, pulling Carol by the hand, headed for where he'd left her horse. He heard the sound of the Pawnee moments later, shouts of rage as they entered the teepee.

They were coming after him and he heard their bodies running through the underbrush as they followed him out the slit he'd cut in the tent. Swerving, he ducked behind a thick-trunked cedar, pushed Carol to the ground in a clump of sweet fennel, and lay down atop her. The Pawnee came by on both sides of the tree, moving too quickly in their haste to find their quarry and ignoring the clump of sweet fennel. As he stayed flattened on the ground over Carol, he could hear the Pawnee chief barking orders. He let the Pawnee go on before he pushed to his feet. He pulled Carol up with him and she followed on his heels as he moved carefully and silently through the cedars, listening to the sounds of the Pawnee just ahead. Changing directions again, he cut between two rows of six-foot-high horseweeds, slowed for a moment to get his bearings, and shifted to the right as he went on.

It took him longer than he wanted to find where he had left Carol's horse, and he had just untied the reins when the shot rang out, smashing into the branch at his elbow. He spun and saw the dark shapes coming toward him. The Pawnee had doubled back and caught sight of him at the horse. "Come on," he said to Carol as he swung onto her horse and pulled her into the saddle in front of him. He sent the horse into a gallop, but immediately had to slow as the trees grew closer together. A half-dozen shots whistled past as he skirted around a pair of cedars, half of them too close for comfort. There was no way he could flatten himself on the horse with Carol in the saddle in front of him and he drew the Colt and fired off a fast volley of shots.

He heard the cries of pain from at least two of the pursuers. The Pawnee sent another cluster of shots at him, but they were wild, and Fargo kept the horse on an erratic path. On foot, the Pawnee were quickly left behind, their next round of shots both short and wide. Fargo searched the darkness, only the moon offering its fitful light as he had to slow to find where he had left the Ovaro. He went left and quickly changed as he realized he'd made a mistake. As he retraced steps, the sounds of the Pawnee faded, and it was at least another three minutes before Fargo found the Ovaro. He skidded Carol's horse to a halt, leaped from the saddle, and flung the Ovaro's reins from the tree branch.

"I want to talk to you," Carol hissed.

"Later," he said.

"Now. We're clear. They've given up," Carol said.

"Hell they have. I insulted the chief. I burned down his teepee," Fargo said and spurred the Ovaro forward. Carol drove her horse after him as he skirted his way through the closely packed cedars. He was finally nearing the open rangeland, where they could make time, when he heard the sound and flung a curse into the air, the soft pounding of un- shod hooves coming up flat behind them. He shot a glance at Carol. When he saw that her horse was al- ready breathing hard, he discarded his plan to make a headlong run for it across the open land. He held to the trees as the Pawnee burst into the open, rac- ing all out across the flatland paralleling the cedars. With no need to dodge and skirt trees, they galloped past where Fargo and Carol moved inside the cedars, the chief at the head of his warriors. He watched the Pawnee go by and let himself hope that they were aimlessly searching.

But the hope vanished as he saw the chief pull up some hundred yards on and his warriors turn al- most as one. Half entering the cedars ahead of where Fargo slowed beside Carol, most of the others turning and entering the trees behind them. The chief and six of his braves halted in the open, a dozen yards from the edge of the tree line. "They saw us," Fargo muttered bitterly as he pulled to a halt. "They have us boxed in. They're in front of us, behind us, and alongside us."

"We're going to be killed and it's all your god- damn fault," Carol spit at him, and he winced at the truth in the accusation, not a complete truth but complete enough. His eyes went to the Pawnee ponies and their riders that filtered through the trees toward them from both sides. There was time only for a last chance and it had to be a final bold- ness, a gauntlet seized and flung down. Death waited anyway, he knew. It was not hard to stare it down. It was not hard because he had no choice. His eyes went to the Pawnee chief and the six braves beside him and he motioned for Carol to follow as he moved the Ovaro slowly out of the trees and into the open. He drew the rifle from its saddle case as the pinto nosed onto the range, putting it to his shoulder and aiming at the Pawnee chief as he halted. The Indian frowned across the few yards at him.

"We will not die alone," Fargo said.

"But you will die," the chief said.

"As will you," Fargo answered. "I will not miss." The Pawnee chief knew it was not an idle threat. The moon afforded more than enough light for accurate shooting. Fargo felt the tiny beads of perspiration form on his forehead and knew how completely he was counting on the power of culture, tradition, and human nature. Inside himself, the Pawnee chief had to react as any man would. He'd have no desire to die in an exchange where dying was certain. Yet he couldn't show fear or weakness, not a Pawnee chief. To do so was to die by disgrace. He had to cast his foe as the one who asked for a way out of the impasse. Inside, the Pawnee chief valued survival as much as lesser men.

The beads of perspiration grew thicker as Fargo hoped he had not miscalculated the complexities of human behavior. He continued to wait, unmoving. He'd win the waiting game, he was certain. He was not the one wrestling with the final decision. He'd cast his dice. Finally, the chief spoke. "You want to find a way to live," he said, his words carefully measured. "That is your last hope." Fargo let a grim smile curl inside him. He had won the first round. The chief had made him appear the one who asked for favors.

"I offer a way, with honor," Fargo said.

"Go on," the chief said.

Fargo fell back on sign language as he lowered the rifle, used the gestures to confirm his words. He made the sign for personal combat. "One to one. I win, the woman and I go free," Fargo said. "No weapons. The chief chooses who fights for the Pawnee." He fell silent and waited again. It was not so simple a challenge as it seemed. It struck at tribal honor, confidence, authority. It was a challenge wrapped in defiance, a dare thrown out with insolence.

"It is done," the chief said. Fargo breathed a deep sigh of relief. Now all he had to do was win, he grunted to himself, all too aware that the end could still be death. "When the sun rises," the chief said. Fargo swore but could only shrug agreement. He had hoped to make the Indian uncomfortable in the moonlight. In general, the Indian did not favor night fighting. Perhaps it had deep roots in tribal beliefs about night and the great spirits. Perhaps it was a result of ingrained, practical ways of life. Perhaps the Indian was lacking in night vision, or simply disliked and distrusted the night. But it was generally true, even to the great warrior Plains tribes. Except for the Apache. But then nothing about the Apache applied to other tribes.

The Pawnee chief slowly swung from his pony, the gesture a kind of seal to the agreement, and his braves formed a wide, loose circle. Fargo motioned to Carol as he dismounted and sat down on the carpet of grama grass. Carol sat down cross-legged beside him and he saw the anger in her hazel eyes. "Are you happy?" she hissed.

"Wouldn't exactly say that," he replied.

"Your damn fault, all of it," she accused.

"It didn't go as I planned," he told her.

"You mean I'm still alive?" she flung back.

"I mean I was going to get to you before they attacked the herd," he explained.

"You made it happen. You told them we were delivering to the army. Why, goddammit, why?" Carol said.

"Decided it was time to strike back for Darcy," he admitted and told her about the rocks dynamited onto her herd.

"For Darcy. How positively gallant," Carol said through her fury.

He glared back. "It seems pretty damn clear who was behind it and everything else that's happened," he said.

"Not to me," she said, and he swore at her adamant stand.

"I'm still giving you the benefit of the doubt," he said. "That's why I wanted to come back for you."

"I'm touched," she said.

"It's past time for lies," he said, ignoring her cutting sarcasm. "It's past time protecting them and it's past time for looking the other way."

"You think that's what I've been doing?" she asked.

"Been wondering," he admitted.

"And that'd make me guilty?" she pressed.

"Morally, if not actually. I'm not sure there's much of a difference," Fargo said. "You telling me something?"

"I'm telling you you can think whatever you like," Carol threw back. He turned from her. She remained intransigent and remained a question mark. But it would all be so much wasted conjecture if he couldn't salvage survival from the specter of death. The moon neared the horizon line, he saw. Dawn was waiting in the wings. So was death.

8

He lay stretched out on the grass, his eyes open only wide enough to take in the dark expanse that was the sky. Carol hadn't spoken and he felt the simmering anger of her as time ticked away. A thin line of pink intruded on the blackness of the sky and Fargo watched it slowly spread, the first long finger of dawn announcing itself. Fargo pushed up to a sitting position and stayed there as the sky began to change. He rose when dawn took command of the earth, and saw the Pawnee chief coming toward him. A tall figure clad only in leather leggings walked beside the chief and led a sturdy-legged pony behind. The chief halted and placed a hand on the younger man's shoulder. Fargo nodded, the gesture unmistakable.

Fargo took in the muscled smoothness of the Pawnee's torso and saw strength and litheness, a body that combined speed and power. He watched the brave flex large, powerful hands at the end of muscular arms. The man's eyes were sharp inside his broad, heavy face. But Fargo caught something else he was glad to see, an arrogance. Undoubtedly earned, it could still be a liability as much as an asset. The chief beckoned with his hands and Fargo undid the gunbelt and lay the Colt on the ground. He pulled the Colt from its saddle case and set it down with the Colt. The chief beckoned again and Fargo took the knife from its calf holster and dropped it beside the guns. But the chief had a surprise for him as the brave climbed onto his pony.

"You begin on your ponies," the chief said and stepped back. Fargo kept his face impassive as he turned and swung onto the Ovaro, but the Pawnee had made his first mistake. He didn't understand the advantage the saddle would give over a bareback rider. Fargo glanced at Carol as she stood back; there was fear and hope mixed in with the anger still in her eyes. He wheeled the Ovaro and faced the Pawnee warrior, who had moved his pony a dozen yards away. As Fargo watched, the Pawnee kicked his mount in the ribs and the horse bolted forward, its rider aiming directly at him. Fargo held the Ovaro in place and gathered his muscles as he saw the Indian racing headlong at him. At the last moment the Pawnee swerved a fraction and hurtled past him, brushing the Ovaro. Fargo saw the Indian strike out with his arm, a clublike, stiff swing. Fargo was going to parry the blow with his own forearm. As he drew back and ducked, he could feel the force of the blow pass over his head; it was given tremendous power by the speed of the pony.

Fargo lifted his arm and tried a glancing blow, but the Indian was out of reach at once. He circled the Ovaro as the Indian turned his pony and charged again. Fargo hunched down in the saddle and prepared to deliver his own blow under the Indian's clublike swing. But as the brave hurtled past, he half rose and twisted his body, kicking out with one leg, the maneuver a brilliant piece of riding and muscle control. Fargo tried to twist away from the unexpected kick and managed to take the full impact of it against his upper arm. But the force of the kick sent him sideways. He would have fallen from the horse had he not grabbed hold of the saddle horn and stopped his fall. He pulled himself up and turned to see the Pawnee was charging again. This time Fargo waited, measuring seconds, and then spun the Ovaro in a tight circle just as the Pawnee reached. The maneuver put too much distance between the horses, and the Indian's stiff-armed swing fell short. But as he went past, Fargo spurred the pinto forward to come alongside the other horse. The Pawnee half turned, surprise flashing through his face as Fargo leaned forward and smashed a straight-arm blow into his back.

The man grunted in pain, yanked his pony away, and made a tight circle, but Fargo sent the Ovaro after him, came alongside him as he circled. The brave reached out, leaning sideways on his pony, and closed one hand around Fargo's outstretched arm. He pulled and Fargo felt the strength of the man's grip. He swung the Ovaro sharply and the Indian had to release his grip or be pulled from his horse. The brave shouted a Pawnee curse, brought his mount around in a tight circle, and charged again. Fargo held the Ovaro in place, his eyes narrowed at the onrushing horse and rider, and he saw the Indian's shoulders and thigh muscles bulge. The man was going to dive from his horse at him and send him flying from the Ovaro and land atop him on the ground.

Fargo waited, his own muscles tensed. The Indian began to rise up on his horse as he neared. Bracing himself, Fargo prepared to flatten himself so that the Pawnee's dive would carry him across the Ovaro's back and cause him to fall on the other side. The Indian pony swerved to brush against the Ovaro and Fargo began to flatten himself. But at the last moment, the Pawnee didn't dive. Instead, he seized his pony by its mane and neck, twisted his body, and kicked out with both feet from his grip on the horse's mane. The acrobatic maneuver had plainly been done countless times and was performed with split-second precision. Realizing he couldn't flatten himself down enough to avoid the kick, Fargo tried to twist sideways, but he was too late. The Pawnee's double kick struck hard and Fargo felt his body shudder. He grabbed for the saddle horn, but his hand slipped away and he felt himself falling from the Ovaro. He managed to twist as he hit the ground. He took most of the fall as he rolled on his shoulders.

He came up on his hands and knees, shook his head to clear it, and pushed to his feet. He headed for the Ovaro to remount, but saw the Pawnee charging at him with his pony, hurtling full-out at him. With a curse, Fargo had time only to dive aside and he felt the horse's legs touch his feet as he was in midair. He hit the ground, rolled, and came up. The Ovaro had skittered a few feet further away, beyond reaching, as the Pawnee had turned and was already charging again. Fargo spread his feet and went into a half crouch, holding his spot as the Indian sent the horse directly at him. Jumping into the air and waving both arms wildly as he let out a tremendous shout, Fargo leaped up directly in front of the horse.

The Indian's mount reacted at once, rearing up in surprise. Horses didn't like the unexpected. The Pawnee went backward, clinging to the horse's rope reins before losing his grip and going off backward over the horse's rump. Fargo was already circling around the Indian pony as the Pawnee hit the ground on his back. Fargo aimed the kick at the man's head and missed as the Indian rolled and leaped to his feet. The Pawnee came at him and Fargo glimpsed the chief and the others moving closer to watch. Fargo shot a straight left at the brave, but the man had the reflexes of a cat; he pulled his head away and brought his own blow down, a short, chopping blow with the side of his hand. Fargo parried it but he could feel the power of the man as pain shot through his forearm.

The Pawnee brought his body low, weaving and leaping forward with a wild left swing that Fargo managed to avoid, readying a counter blow as the man pulled back. But the Pawnee didn't pull back. Instead, he stayed low, dived, and barreled into Fargo with both arms wrapping around his foe. Fargo went back and down with the unexpected force of the attack. The Pawnee's big hands were instantly at his throat. Fargo grasped the man's wrists and tried to pry his grip loose, but he quickly saw that it would be like prying a vise open. The Indian's powerful hands were already cutting off his air to him. Drawing his legs up, Fargo dug his heels into the ground, using his powerful back muscles to lift himself upward with the Indian clinging to him. Twisting, he threw himself sideways. When he felt the man's grip finally loosen, Fargo brought a short but hard blow into his ribs. The Indian grunted and fell away.

Fargo spun and, still half on his knees, tossed a long, looping right as the Pawnee started to push to his feet. The blow caught the man on the point of his jaw with enough force to send him sprawling backward. On his feet, Fargo rushed forward. He managed to twist, but couldn't avoid taking an upward kick from the Pawnee's right leg against his hip, which sent pain shooting through his leg. The Pawnee had scooted back enough to regain his feet and came forward again, his black eyes burning with hate. He tried another long left, followed with a right, and Fargo easily parried both blows, but then he erupted in a whirling, twisting, spinning succession of blows and kicks that seemed to come from every direction at once. Fargo ducked and twisted away and parried, finally flying backward from the speed of the human windmill that came at him.

Pausing only a moment, the Indian began another series of the spinning, whirling punches and kicks, and Fargo let himself go backward again. He made a few feeble efforts to counterpunch but spent most of his time retreating and ducking blows. But his eyes were on more than the Pawnee's kicks and blows. They searched the man's face and saw the arrogance grow in it and become reckless confidence. The Pawnee came at him again as a whirling dervish and Fargo again gave ground, seemingly able only to defend himself, when suddenly he halted and ducked away from a swiping blow. Then he lashed out with a left that exploded as if it had been fired from a cannon. It caught the Pawnee flush on the jaw and he staggered, his whirling arms suddenly flopping loosely. Fargo followed with a right that snapped the Indian's head around and sent him sprawling. He hit the ground, turned, and came to his feet, but his eyes were glazed. Fargo sank a hard left and right into the man's abdomen. The brave went down on both knees and doubled over, hands clutching his midsection.

Fargo's left hook straightened him up and sent him onto his back. Following up instantly, Fargo leaped forward, took the man's head in an armlock, and began to tighten his grip. He glanced up at the circle of faces watching him and relaxed his hold. He let the Pawnee's head fall limply, silently, to one side. He stood up and the brave dropped onto the ground, unconscious. Fargo stepped back and gestured and three of the Pawnee came forward to pick up the limp form and carry him away. Fargo moved forward, toward the chief, his eyes meeting the man's stare. There was no need for words on either man's part. The chief slowly turned his back on Fargo, pulled himself onto his pony, and walked away, the others following. It was over. Fargo let a deep sigh escape him as he walked to where he'd left his weapons.

He had just finished putting away the throwing knife when Carol came to him. "That was pretty damn wonderful," she said.

"How wonderful?" he grunted.

"All the way wonderful. But it doesn't change what you did, if that's what you're asking," Carol said.

"It doesn't change what I feel, either," he said. "Get your horse and let's move."

She retrieved her mount and swung in alongside him as he began to ride slowly across the range. The day was nearing an end when they reached Carol's place. "Maybe you'd better look up your friends and tell them you're alive," he said.

"I'll have to tell them why, and why it all happened," Carol said.

"Doesn't bother me any," Fargo said.

"Because you're convinced they were behind the attacks," she said. He nodded.

"You're still the question mark. I want to know

how deep down that hardness inside you goes," he said.

"There's a meeting at our hall night after tomorrow," she said. "Come. Talk to them yourself, to all of us."

"You thinking they're going to up and confess?" he asked.

"No, but you can question them. Maybe you'll get a different picture. Maybe you won't. It's worth a try."

"Maybe. I'll think on it. You're still the only one I want to know about," Fargo said.

"Try believing me," Carol said.

"I might have once. Not now. Too much has happened. It's past time for just believing. I want more," he said.

"You want what I can't give you," she said.

"Or won't," he finished, and she looked both hurt and resentful. He left her and rode away in the dusk, the conflict of emotions still churning inside him. He swung onto the road that led to Darcy's place as the dusk began to turn into dark, slowing to a halt as the buckboard came toward him. Even before he took note of the driver he saw the heavy, special iron grips on both sides of the seat. His eyes went to Sid Bundy at the reins, his tight, bitter face in a sneer as he slowed.

"Look who's back," Bundy said.

"In person," Fargo said.

"I heard they almost finished her, would have except for you," Sid Bundy said.

"How'd you hear?" Fargo asked quickly.

"Went to town, like I am now. She's been talking," the man said.

"You saying you think they're the ones?" Fargo queried.

"Who else?" Bundy shrugged.

"You've got reason enough. You hate her," Fargo said.

"You forgettin' something?" Bundy said.

"The wheelchair?"

"Bull's-eye. How's a man in a wheelchair going to get around to her in the mountains?" Bundy snorted.

"Hire guns," Fargo suggested.

Bundy made a wry sound. "It costs money to hire guns," he said.

"Speaking of getting around, I know how you get into the buckboard from the wheelchair but how do you get the buckboard hitched?" Fargo questioned.

"A neighbor's kid comes by, does it for me, then drives it out where I can bring the chair alongside it," Bundy said. "Any more questions?"

"Not now," Fargo said. Sid Bundy snapped the reins on the horse and drove on. Fargo watched him go into the night as he turned the man's words in his mind. Bundy was right in that hiring guns cost money. Killers didn't come cheap, especially ones who'd set fires and dynamite rocks. But Fargo remembered Darcy saying that the association paid him hush money once a month. His brow furrowed, he turned the pinto from the road and headed for the pyramid rock and the river behind Sid Bundy's house. It was time for a closer look at Bundy's place while he had the chance.

He reached the house. The moonlight was glinting on the river behind it. He pulled up in the front yard and dismounted. Bundy's wheelchair was standing where he'd halted it. He locked the brake and pulled himself into the buckboard. It was obviously the way he always did it, his own routine. The boy would bring the buckboard from the stable and go his way. Then Bundy would wheel himself from the house and pull himself into the wagon. Fargo began to move toward the house. There were no outdoor lanterns and an overhanging hackberry cast a shadow that turned the area into almost complete darkness.

Fargo walked toward the house when suddenly he felt himself pitch forward, his feet going out from under him. He landed on his hands and knees, and saw he'd stepped into a ditch that ran along the front of the house. He pushed to his feet, brushed himself off, and went on to Bundy's house where the doorway had been flattened to allow easy access for the wheelchair. He pushed the door open, saw the lamp on inside the house, and stepped into the room. He moved quickly through the house, taking the kerosene lamp with him, ignoring most of the clutter and slowing when he reached what was plainly Sid Bundy's bedroom. It was more ordered than the other rooms. There was plenty of space alongside the bed to maneuver a wheelchair, with a large window affording a good view of the river behind the house. A dresser took up one wall and Fargo opened the drawers; they held little, just a few clothes. He pulled out the last bottom drawer and stared down at the metal box inside it.

Bringing it out of the drawer, he set it on the bed and lifted the cover. Inside, he saw some twenty envelopes, each filled with bills, and the furrow crossed his brow as he stared at the money. It confirmed Darcy's words about the regular payments, but it did more than that. It's very neatness seemed to say that this was money received and put aside untouched. If that were so, it hadn't been used to buy hired killers and that seemed to take Sid Bundy out of the picture. Fargo realized he should be taking satisfaction in one more finger pointed at Dave Cord and the others. It bolstered his own conclusions. Yet Fargo frowned and knew he didn't feel satisfaction. For some reason he couldn't pinpoint, Bundy continued to nag at him more than ever. He swore to himself, carefully put the tin box back in the drawer, and made his way from the house. He took care not to fall over the ditch this time, swung onto the Ovaro, and rode away.

He rode through the dark to Darcy's place and was surprised to find that the sharp odor of burned wood still hung in the air. He crossed through the hawthorns to Darcy's large cabin, where he saw lamps burning brightly inside. Darcy came to the door as Fargo paused, his eyes slowly scanning the front of the cabin, narrowing as he peered into the windows, then taking in the high brush alongside the cabin and the trees close to the front. "Aren't you coming in?" Darcy asked. He broke off his thoughtful scanning of the house and went into the cabin. She followed, hands on hips as she held him with a jaundiced stare. "You did it," she said. "I heard the Pawnee scattered their entire herd."

"That's right," Fargo said.

"You save her neck, too?" Darcy questioned.

"Took a lot more doing than I planned," he said.

"She properly grateful?"

"I wouldn't exactly say that," he said.

Darcy studied him a moment and decided not to pursue the answer. "You sure as hell have seen enough now to know who's been behind the attacks on me," she said.

"I know how it looks. I still want more, some final proof," Fargo said.

"Dammit, you talk about wanting proof but I think all you want is a way to find her innocent," Darcy shot back.

"That's not so," he protested even as he knew she had touched a raw place. "I get what I want, it could find her guilty," he added, and she gave him a skeptical glare. "I've a way to do it," he said. "It'll take your help." She didn't answer and frowned back at him. "Or maybe you're more interested in accusing than truth," he said, throwing a barb of his own.

"That's not fair," she said. "I'm the one they've been trying to kill. I've a right to accuse."

"Then help me," he said.

"I'm listening," she said after a moment.

"Can you disappear, hole up somewhere for a night?" he asked.

"There's a cave I used to use when I hunted lynx," she said.

"You've a back door to this place you can sneak out of?" he asked.

"Yes."

"I'm going to set you up to be killed, only you won't be here," he said. "I'm going to tell Carol something. She'll be the only one who'll know. I'll be here waiting. If there's an attack I'll see who it is and I'll know only Carol could have told them."

"Proof," Darcy murmured.

"Enough for me," he agreed.

"And if there's no attack, if nobody comes?" Darcy asked.

"That'll be proof, too, another kind," he said.

Darcy was silent a long moment, her lips tight. "I

guess so," she conceded. "But it has to be done right. It'll be no good if they come, smell a setup, and leave. You still won't be satisfied."

"That's true," he said.

"I should be here, let them see me," Darcy said. "That's the only way it'll work."

"No. That'd be too risky. I couldn't save you from a bullet. I'll rig up a dummy that'll make them think it's you here. I'll put the lamp on low. It'll work."

"Maybe and maybe not. It could all go for nothing. I don't like it," Darcy said.

"I'll make it work," he said, but she continued to look dubious.

"When?" she asked.

"Tell you when I come by next. You just get yourself ready to hole up. Meanwhile, you stay here," he said. She nodded, still unhappily, and went to the door with him. Her eyes searched his face.

"I wish I could decide," she said.

"About what?"

"Whether to hate you or love you," she said.

"This can decide that, too," he told her, and then swung onto the Ovaro and rode away. A mile on, he found a spot to bed down under a stand of post oak and stretched out. His plan was the only way to find the truth and nail down the proof he wanted to satisfy himself and Darcy. Her conclusions were too certain. His were too uncertain. It was the only way, he told himself again. It took him a while to sleep, his thoughts filled with Dave Cord, Ed Buckley, Amos Stockel, and Carol. But Sid Bundy still intruded, still refused dismissal for reasons that eluded him, Fargo pondered. Was he just clinging to slim possibilities out of caution, Fargo asked himself, or was he missing something about Sid Bundy. There had to be a reason why Bundy stayed with him, even though he couldn't give it form or shape. He finally fell asleep swearing at all of them.

9

When morning came, Fargo found a pond, and washed and breakfasted on a stand of wild cherry as he solidified his plans. His first stop was in town, a visit to Lola at the Bottle, Beef, and Bed. He expected a certain amusement at his request and the madam didn't disappoint him. "You don't look the type to wear a wig, big boy," she said, giving a soft chuckle.

"Shows you can't ever tell about people," he growled. "I'm sure you keep a stock of them on hand."

"We do. Sometimes a girl just can't get her hair looking good. Any special color?" Lola asked.

"Brown, in the brunette range," Fargo said. Lola motioned for him to wait and returned in a few minutes with a wig, which he saw at once was much too long and full. "I know you sometimes keep wigs on a headstand. Would you happen to have one?" he asked.

She cocked her head at him. "Cost you another three bucks and me a lot of curiosity," the woman said.

"Get it. A hatbox, too," Fargo said. She returned with the headstand and he wedged the stand and the wig into the hatbox, paid her, and started from the dance hall.

"You'll look lovely in it, honey," Lola called to him

144

and he made a gesture to her as he left, her laughter following him. His next stop was the general store, where he brought two broomsticks, a coat hanger, and a scissors. It was noon when he arrived at Darcy's place, his eyes again scanning the brush and trees around the cabin. He brought all his purchases inside and she said nothing as she watched him take the scissors to the wig and trim it down closer to the way she wore her hair. He began to build the dummy, using the headstand, the coat hanger, and the cut-down broomsticks.

"I want one of your blouses," he said. She took off the one she wore and he stopped to look at the high, round, sassy breasts with the tiny pink nipples. She handed him the blouse with defiance in her eyes, pushed the high breasts forward as she stood very straight. "You saying something?" he asked.

"Might be," she said.

"What?"

"I'm saying this won't work. Let me stay and I'll make you glad you did," Darcy said.

"No. You won't make me glad I did when you've taken a bullet," he said. "It'll work well enough with the lamp on low."

Crossly, she pulled another blouse from a peg and put it on and came to lean against his chest. "I want this to work. I want you to get your proof. You won't believe me till you do and I want you to believe me."

"I'll get it," he said and stepped back to survey his handiwork. The dummy sat in a stuffed chair, visible only from the chest up, back to the door. The wig hung on the headstand, the coat hanger forming shoulders on which the blouse hung. The cut-down broomsticks filled out the sides of the blouse. "It'll do it," he said. "In the dim light it'll do it."

"What if they wait and watch. They'll expect me to move, walk around," Darcy said.

"They'll think you dozed off in the chair," Fargo said and she shook her head in disagreement. "Now, I'm going to pay Carol a visit. It'll be dark when I get back. You stay in the cabin and sneak out the back door after dark. Go to your cave and stay holed up till morning."

"Where will you be?" Darcy asked.

"Somewhere outside, waiting, watching. Their first shot will be their last one," he said and left her still looking distinctly unhappy. He cut across a low hill to reach Carol's place and she came out as he rode to a halt. "Just passing by," he said as he admired her cool, slender figure, her hazel eyes regarding him with that one perpetually raised eyebrow. She looked completely contained and in charge of anything that came her way. "Just passing by," he said. "Stopped at Darcy's."

"Of course," she said disdainfully.

"Your friends didn't get their way," he said.

"You're assuming, again," Carol said.

"Maybe, but she's not giving in to anything that's happened. She's alone at her place, making plans to hire new hands and bring in more mustangs and go on bigger than ever," Fargo said.

"Once a hardnose always a hardnose," Carol said and he thought he caught a note of grudging admiration in her voice.

"Just thought you'd like to know," he said. She shrugged and watched him ride on. He didn't circle until he was out of sight of the ranch and he rode slowly, letting the time drift on. When he found himself drawing near Sid Bundy's place, he turned away. He didn't want Sid Bundy intruding on his thoughts and his concentration. When the day slid to an end, Fargo took the pinto to Darcy's cabin. He tethered the horse deep in the hawthorns, went into the cabin, and put the lamp on low, leaving quickly and pausing to peer in through the window from the tall brush. He was still very satisfied. Darcy seemed to be in the chair, everything draping properly. The figure did seem a little stiff and unmoving, he admitted, but he counted on any attackers moving quickly once they glimpsed the figure in the chair. He found a spot in the high brush that let him see the entire front of the cabin and the hawthorns facing it. Lying on his stomach, he held the Colt in his hand and watched the moon slowly curve over the cabin.

If the attack came it would be proof he'd been right all along in suspecting Dave Cord and the others. But it would be a bitter vindication, he realized, thinking about Carol. He found himself hoping there'd be no attack. It would be the only thing that could clear Carol. She could still have looked the other way but it'd show her involvement was passive more than active. It'd be a small victory but he'd settle for small victories. It had come down to that. But his wandering thoughts were almost instantly shattered as he felt the hairs of his neck grow stiff. His skin tingled. He was not alone.

He lay still, hardly breathing as he strained his ears. The sound came to him soon enough, the soft brush of leaves being moved ever so carefully. From the hawthorns. They were in the hawthorns, creeping forward. The sound came again, closer but still in the hawthorns. Another sound interrupted, sharper, harsher. His glance went to the cabin window and he saw the shape move by the chair and stand in front of the dummy figure and turn and stand alone. He felt his throat go dry. *Goddamn,* he swore, the words sticking inside him, *goddamn.* He stared in horror and disbelief at Darcy as she moved around the cabin. She had come in through the rear door, he realized and felt both fury and despair rise inside him. His eyes darted to the hawthorns, where he could see the flicker of movement and the dark, shadowed figure.

The shot exploded just as he leaped to his feet, crashing through the window and he uttered a groan of anguish as he saw Darcy go down. He emptied his pistol into the hawthorns as he ran to the cabin, knew he was spraying bullets, intent only on making the shooter in the hawthorns duck away. He crashed into the cabin, hit the floor and crawled to where Darcy lay beside the chair. She was breathing and he saw a trickle of blood along the side of her temple. But the shot had only grazed her and as he turned, still on the cabin floor, he heard the sound of a horse galloping away. He rose to one knee, cursing as he sighed in relief and turned to Darcy. She moaned as he sat her up. Her eyes flickered and stared at him.

"Stubborn little fool," he hissed, relief tempering fury. "You damn near got yourself killed." He took a kerchief and cleaned the trickle of blood from her temple and saw that she had only flesh wounds and his anger took charge. "I had to lay down a wild barrage to stop them from shooting and they got away, dammit. You ever follow orders?" he half shouted.

"I wanted it to work," she said, almost contritely.

"It would have, more than it did now," he flung back.

"You have your answer. That's what you wanted," Darcy said.

"I wanted to bring down at least one of them, nail it shut," he said.

"You've enough. She told them and they followed through," Darcy said.

"Or sent somebody," he said and she frowned back. "Didn't really hear more than one horse," he said.

"Makes no difference. You set it up. They took the bait. What more do you want?"

"Nothing," he said grimly, aware that she was right. He helped her stand and she swayed and fell against him.

"I'm feeling weak, dizzy. I'd better lie down," she said.

"It's called shock, physical and emotional. Almost getting killed can do that to you," he said without gentleness and helped her to the bed in the next room. She lay down, but her arms stayed around him and he lay down beside her and helped her as she shrugged off clothes and brought her firm, compact body to him. He shed his shirt and boots and held her as she trembled. She grew still after a few moments and fell asleep. He lay awake with her and wished he could feel as contented as she looked.

He had what he wanted, as she had told him. It had worked. He had the proof. But he felt no elation, no sense of victory, not even the comfort of a job well down. He didn't have to ask himself why. Winning was not always sweet. Finally he let his eyes close and he slept holding her until the new day came to flood the room with sunlight. She awoke and he watched as

149

she used a basin to wash. He enjoyed the loveliness of her high sassy breasts moving almost in unison, her compact figure radiating an energetic beauty all its own. She pulled on her clothes and went outside and made coffee and biscuits as he washed and dressed.

"When are you going to go get them?" Darcy asked after they'd finished the meal.

"Been thinking about that," he said. "I'm no marshal. I can't arrest them. I'm going to have to bring Sheriff Bailey to do that."

Her eyes narrowed at him. "I don't like something I'm hearing in your voice," Darcy said.

"They'll deny everything, of course. They wouldn't be able to if I'd nailed one of them," he said and saw the spots of color come to her cheeks.

"You tell me he won't take them in?" Darcy said.

"He's in their pockets, you've said. He could weasel out of doing anything," Fargo said.

"Son of a bitch," Darcy muttered.

"I'll try a different approach. I won't bring Bailey in yet. They're all meeting at their town hall tonight. I'll pay a visit. Maybe I'll find something more. Maybe one of my shots winged someone. If not, then I'll go to Bailey and make the case best as I can," Fargo said.

"Tell him there's nobody else but them," Darcy said almost despairingly.

"He'll point to Bundy, just as I've done."

"Use Bundy's answer to you. It's solid. How's a man in a wheelchair going to get around to do all these things?" she said.

"I'll use it, and whatever else I can," Fargo said. "If it doesn't work, maybe I can find a way around Sheriff Bailey."

"And maybe you can't," Darcy said, her face tight.

"I'm not taking that chance. Two can play at their games."

"What's that mean?" he asked.

"Whatever," she said sullenly as she turned away. He knew he wasn't going to get any other answer. He went outside, saddled the Ovaro, and was ready to ride when she came out, her face still wrapped in sullen anger.

"I'll stop by later tonight and tell you where we stand," he said. He wanted to reassure her in some way, aware how she still harbored suspicions he was sympathetic to Carol. "I'm not backing off," he said.

"That's nice," she said flatly and he had the distinct feeling she was past caring. He rode away feeling unsatisfied and let the pinto find its own way across the hillsides, stopping to stretch out beside a stream and let himself marshal his arguments for the sheriff. It was going to come down to that, he feared. His visit to the association meeting was a fishing expedition at most, and he was concerned at what Carol would read in his face. She'd be looking, searching, probing for the unsaid, he knew. He wondered if he could mask his anger at her. Finally, as the day drew to a close, he returned to the saddle and walked the pinto across the low hills.

He continued to think about the meeting he'd have with the sheriff. He'd have no hesitation tossing Sid Bundy's question at Bailey and he let it all swim back over him. How's a man in a wheelchair going to get around riding, shooting, and leading attacks? The question begged itself and stayed in his mind as he rode through the dusk when suddenly he yanked the horse to a stop. The question spiraled through him again, the same but different and suddenly he had another answer, the explanation for Sid Bundy's continued nagging intrusion into his thoughts. The unexplained suddenly had an explanation. The subconscious persistent prodding suddenly had broken forth into the conscious mind. Reasons had taken shape and form.

With a curse, he sent the Ovaro into a gallop, turning north and finally racing past the pyramid rock and up the rise of land that led to Sid Bundy's house. Bundy was in his wheelchair as Fargo raced up, just outside the flattened entranceway to the house. "Shit, you again?" Bundy rasped as Fargo swung from the saddle.

"For the last time," Fargo said as he approached Bundy. "Got one more question for you." He yanked the Colt from its holster and leveled it at Sid Bundy. "Move. Ride that wheelchair across the ground out front," he said.

"You gone crazy?" Bundy frowned.

"Move it," Fargo snapped and the man glared at him as he began to wheel the chair forward. Fargo walked alongside him. "Keep going," he ordered.

"What the hell's all this about?" Bundy demanded.

"I told you, one more question, a variation on yours," Fargo said. He put one hand on the back of the wheelchair and gave it a push. Bundy yelled as the wheelchair sped forward faster than he was pushing it.

"No, don't, goddammit," Bundy screamed.

"Faster," Fargo shouted and pushed the chair again. Bundy increased his pushing motion to get control of the chair that rolled headlong across the ground. Fargo, only a half step behind, saw Bundy close his hands around the brake, press hard, and bring the chair to a halt only inches from the ditch. "Go on," Fargo ordered.

"Can't, goddammit," Bundy said, his eyes filling with alarm.

"Sure you can. Watch," Fargo said, and stepping behind the wheelchair, he lifted and upended it. Bundy spilled forward out of the chair, throwing his arms up to protect his face as he hit the ground inches from the ditch.

"You goddamn gone crazy," Bundy screamed as he lay on his side, his legs drawn up uselessly. "Fucking madman. What the hell's wrong with you?"

"Watch again," Fargo said, and he proceeded to unlock the brake on the wheelchair and send the chair rolling. The two wheels hit the ditch and it nosed over instantly. "Look at that," Fargo said. "Now, here's my question. How does a man in a wheelchair cross over a ditch the chair can't make? How does he reach the buckboard on the other side?" Bundy's eyes narrowed and filled with hate as he stared up from his side. "Answer. He gets out of the chair, lifts it across the ditch, then gets back in the chair and rolls to the buckboard in case anyone comes by while he's getting in," Fargo said and leaned forward. "Now, you get up, you clever bastard. The act's over."

"You're crazy. You've gone out of your goddamn head," Bundy said, but there was a trapped animal look to him now. "I'm going to have you in jail for this."

Fargo jumped up and came down on the tilted wheelchair with both feet. The wheels caved in, the arms broke and fell off and the back collapsed. "You can add destroying a wheelchair," Fargo said. "Get up, dammit."

"I can't," Bundy insisted.

"Then I'm going to have to kick you all the way to town. You sure won't be able to walk then," Fargo said and moved toward the man. He didn't know if Bundy had the guts and the strength to keep to his act in the face of real punishment and decided not to find out. Bundy knew he was already trapped. He'd seize a chance to break out and turn it all around. Fargo halted beside him, drew back one leg, and kicked out. But he made it an awkward kick that left himself off balance. Bundy saw his chance and responded with the speed of a rattler spotting a meal. He struck out with both hands, wrapped them around Fargo's off-balance right leg, and pulled. Fargo went down, but he'd expected to and he managed to let himself fall loosely instead of stiffening. He brought a short right up in a truncated arc and drove it into Sid Bundy's ribs. The man grunted, fell away, and rolled, leaping to his feet. He rushed forward, his face a snarling mask of rage. Fargo went backward, avoided a lunging right, and then a left. He ducked low and brought up his own left hook, putting all his strength behind it.

Bundy's head snapped back and he staggered, emitted a roar and lowered his head to plunge forward in a half leap, half dive. Fargo twisted his body away from the lunge, and smashed a short, brutal punch into Bundy's body as the man flew by. He heard a rib crack as Bundy fell and groaned and tried to turn back for another lunge, but Fargo's left and right cross all but took his head off. He fell sprawling, and rolled over. He pulled himself up and tried to weave forward. A short left sent him down again and he lay there, gasping in pain. "Want another try?" Fargo asked.

"No," Bundy managed to say and Fargo pulled him up by the shoulder.

"It almost worked for you," Fargo said. "You fooled everybody."

"The little bitch deserved to die. She almost killed me. It wasn't any of her doing that I came out of it," Bundy said.

"And saw your chance. Nobody knew you weren't a cripple," Fargo said. "You masterminded everything that happened to Darcy and knew the association would be blamed, by Darcy and most anyone else. Why'd you want to get back at them, too?"

"They thought I'd be happy with that measly little bit of money they doled out to me every month. I told them I deserved more but they laughed at me. I got them at each other's throats. I figured when I finally finished off Darcy I'd find a way to let them get the blame for it."

"All for your twisted revenge," Fargo said, and stepping to the Ovaro, he took his lariat down. He tied Bundy's hand and foot and half walked and half dragged him to his house and strapped him to the small tree alongside the entranceway.

"She surprised me about one thing," Bundy said.

"Who?"

"Darcy Ingram. She took a lot, suspected Dave Cord and the others all along, but she never hit back at them. I was waiting to see that, thought she'd do it before this," Bundy said and Fargo stared at the man. He listened to Sid Bundy but it was Darcy he was hearing. *Two can play at their games*, she had said and refused any more of an answer.

He spun and raced for the Ovaro and vaulted into the saddle. That moment Bundy had waited for had come. He sent the horse into an all-out gallop and wondered if he were already too late to stop one more terrible mistake, an error none would ever recover from, most of all Darcy. He raced through the night and cursed the fact that, through none of his own doing, Sid Bundy could have the last laugh. Ironically, Darcy could give him the triumph he wanted. The Ovaro ran full-out as Fargo drove the horse to use every ounce of his powerful fore-and-hindquarters. Flattening himself in the saddle to reduce wind resistance, Fargo sent the Ovaro across a shortcut that few horses could negotiate without slowing to a canter. But the Ovaro didn't drop a moment of speed and Fargo straightened up as they reached the edge of town. He kept the horse racing through the darkened streets.

He only slowed when he reached the meeting hall, pulling the pinto to a halt as he leaped from the saddle. The first thing he saw was the piece of two-by-four wedged against the door to the hall, preventing it from being pushed open from inside. The next thing he noticed were the still-wet stains around the lower edges of the wooden buildings. His nostrils drew in the sharp odor of kerosene. He started toward the door to pull away the two-by-four when, from the side of the building, the flame exploded into the air. He fell backward as the flame shot around the other side, fed by the kerosene that had been tossed onto the structure.

It was then that Darcy came around the corner of the hall, a length of still-burning lucifer in one hand. Her eyes widened as she saw him. "No, no, goddammit," Fargo swore and winced as he saw the wood of the building catch instant fire. In seconds, the outer walls of the meeting hall were ablaze with flame that raced to the roof. "They're not getting away with what they've done and they're not going to do anymore," Darcy said.

Fargo ran to the front door and had to fall back from the heat of the flames. It would only take minutes for the interior of the hall to become an oven, he knew, and he could hear those inside pounding futilely at the door. He ran past Darcy to the Ovaro. There was no time for explanations. There was time only for desperate action where every second counted. Taking the lariat, he ran back to the meeting hall that was now entirely engulfed in flames, flung the rope across the tall piece of two-by-four, where it clung for a moment and then fell to the ground. But one end of it lay on the other side of the wood wedge. Pulling his hat down and keeping his head low, he darted forward. He could feel the tremendous heat of the flames as he neared the building. Staying low, he reached out, grabbed hold of the other end of the lariat, and ran back with it in his hand.

Twisting the two ends of the rope together, he vaulted onto the Ovaro, wrapped the lariat around the saddle horn, and sent the horse bolting forward. He felt the wedged piece of wood come loose and crash down to the ground as he pulled it away from the door. Leaping from the saddle, he saw the figures stumble out of the building, half falling, half running through the gauntlet of flames. Running forward, he saw Carol go down on one knee. He lifted her up as he ran from the flame-engulfed doorway with her. He lowered her to the ground away from the burning building, where she gasped in air as she rested on her elbows. He saw Dave Cord coughing hard but drawing in enough air; the others were doing the same as they lay on the ground.

Fargo straightened up and faced Darcy as she came forward, her face tight. "You had to come save her. I don't understand you," Darcy said. "After all they've done and her a part of it."

"It was Sid Bundy," Fargo said. Darcy stared at him, the frown gathering on her forehead and he saw disbelief and protest in her eyes. "I've got him tied up at his place," Fargo said and saw Carol and the others sit up, their eyes on him. "The wheelchair was an act. He can walk, run, ride, and shoot. He was behind everything that happened. He planned on getting back at all of you."

"My God," Darcy breathed, shock seizing her face as she stared openmouthed at him.

"Thinking about how you almost incinerated a half-dozen innocent people?" Fargo pushed at her.

"I'm going to be sick," Darcy said. She turned away and dropped to her knees, all the color drained from her face.

"Her damn fault, all of it," Carol said.

"Her accusing us of everything all this time," Dave Cord chimed in.

Fargo turned to them. "Don't you go getting righteous. You started it when you used Bundy, made a pawn of him to trap Darcy into sending her herd through his place. It backfired, but more than you know. None of you have clean hands." He looked at Carol and then at Darcy, and the stubborn tilts of both their chins. "Maybe you deserve each other," he said. He started to turn away when the night shuddered with a large hissing noise and he turned back to see the building collapse in on itself. It seemed somehow terribly fitting.

He climbed onto the Ovaro as the others watched in silence. "Get your sheriff to bring in Bundy. You can all press charges against him," Fargo said. He sent the pinto forward at a walk and didn't look back. He rode into the night until he stopped at a cluster of bur oak and bedded down. He slept quickly, wanting to wipe away the sour taste in his mouth. It was well into the new morning when he woke. After washing at a stream and dressing, he started out on the Ovaro. He let him set his own slow pace. He wandered down a slope when the two riders appeared. They came immediately toward him and pulled up together. Darcy spoke first, after a motion by Carol.

"We've been looking for you," she said. "We figured you'd be too tired to go far."

"We thought about what you said about deserving each other," Carol said. "We think it's a good idea. We'll change our ways in the association, from how we treat our wild stock to how we sell to our customers. Darcy will come in with us and be head of operations. She has a way with mustangs."

"I suppose I ought to say congratulations," Fargo said.

"In short, we won't be so greedy and Darcy won't be so righteous," Carol said.

"We want you to ride trail for us, come in with us," Darcy said.

He put his head back and laughed before he answered. "Thanks but no thanks," he said.

"Why not?" Carol frowned.

"You can put away your differences and that'll be

good but there's one thing you can't put away," he said.

"What's that?" Darcy asked.

"Your jealousy," Fargo said.

"You underestimate us," Carol said.

"I do? All right, if I come in with you, who do I screw first?" he asked.

"Me," they both said and frowned at each other.

"Good day, ladies, and good luck," Fargo said and sent the Ovaro into a trot.

"You'd have a hell of a good time," Darcy called after him.

"Don't doubt it," he called back and rode over the crest of a hill. There were invitations you couldn't turn down and there were those you had better.

LOOKING FORWARD!
The following is the opening
section from the next novel in the exciting
***Trailsman* series from Signet:**

THE TRAILSMAN #194

MONTANA STAGE

It began in Montana,
in the Beaverhead foothills,
the strange story of the vanishing
stagecoach, where death and greed
were the unseen passengers . . .

The big man snapped his eyes open and let a soft oath escape his lips as the sudden clatter intruded upon the peaceful quiet of the glen. He sat up in the thicket of yellow-flowered hop cover, his hand automatically dropping to the butt of the big Colt at his hip. His lake blue eyes peered up at the road that ran alongside the tall sandstone rocks some fifty yards away and as he watched, the stagecoach burst into view. A four-horse team running all-out and driverless, sent the coach careening wildly along the curves of the road.

"Shit," he swore aloud as he leaped to his feet and saw the stage gather even more speed on a short stretch of straight road. No mud wagon or light-bodied coach, he saw, but a full Concord with a front and rear boot, the classic of stagecoaches, the finest of the coachmaker's art and the heart of transportation in this wild land.

Running forward, Skye Fargo dug his heels into the firm ground as he ran to where the Ovaro grazed on a field of panic grass, made a vaulting leap into the saddle, and sent the horse into an instant gallop. A quick glance at the stagecoach let him see the wagon careening on two wheels as it disappeared around a curve. He hadn't seen any passengers but they were probably at the bottom of the coach, clinging on for dear life or perhaps already knocked unconscious. When he neared the rocks, Fargo kept the Ovaro just below the road along a flat stretch as he galloped past the coach. Seeing a narrow passage appear to his left, he sent the pinto into it and let it take him up to the road just as the four-horse team came thundering around the curve. Slowing, Fargo let the runaway horses pass him on the narrow width of road. When the coach came abreast of him, keeping his thighs tight around the horse, he leaned out and closed one hand on the iron rail that rimmed the driver's seat.

Gathering every muscle in his powerful body, he half leaped, half pulled himself through the air, twisting his body as he did. Slamming into the side of the coach, he got an arm around the iron rail, then a leg, and flung himself sideways onto the driver's seat. Turning, he saw the next curve coming up, the stage rocking back and forth from side to side. It wouldn't make the sharpness of the curve, he knew, and he grabbed hold of the wildly flapping reins. He pulled hard on the two outside horses, making them turn in and slow the other two. The team began to rein in as he took the curve, slowing enough to negotiate the dangerous bend. Pulling steadily, he continued to slow the heavy stagecoach as it came out of the curve and finally brought it to a halt on a straight stretch of the road.

The horses blew air as they breathed hard, glad to end their panic-stricken, headlong flight. Fargo swung from the coach and pulled the door open. The furrow dug into his brow as he stared into the stage and saw the emptiness that greeted him. Possibilities leaped into his head at once. Had the horses bolted when the passengers had been outside, he wondered. Had they been thrown out during the wild ride? Or had the stage been empty all along. The last didn't sit right. Nobody ran an empty stage across this territory. It didn't pay to go without a stage at least half full. He went to the front boot and pulled the canvas aside. A single suitcase stared back at him from inside the boot. He moved past the stage to check the rear boot, where he saw a woman's traveling bag. But the two pieces were enough to tell him there had been passengers. Returning to the body of the coach, he leaned inside and spied the handkerchief on the floor, wedged against the inner door.

Small, with an embroidered border, it was unquestionably a woman's handkerchief. Two passengers definitely, probably more, Fargo guessed. But what had happened to them? He couldn't go back looking for them. The stage could have come from anywhere in the territory. But the thought slid through his mind. If he couldn't find where it had been, maybe he could find out where it was going. His eyes went to the team. Horses that pulled a stage on a regular run quickly learned the route, often better than many a driver. They could go it on their own with a combination of memory and instinct. He surveyed the horses and saw that they had calmed down, though two were still lathered. Pulling himself into the driver's seat of the stage, he took the reins again and gave the team the order to move with a gentle touch. They went on and he kept them at a walk, then at a slow trot, then he sat back and let the team go on without direction from him.

The Ovaro followed along, as he knew it would, and Fargo watched the horses move along the road between the sandstone rocks. When the road moved downward, it turned onto scrub brush prairie land and came to another road, Fargo sat up straight as the horses unhesitatingly took the second road. He held the reins loosely and the team went down the second road that cut across land studded with clusters of burr oak and rock. The road led over a stretch of plains heavy with gray-green sagebrush and when another road appeared he watched the horses take it without even slowing. Flocks of crows and Bullock's orioles flew overhead as the stage went on and Fargo saw two lakes in the distance. The road rose into low, rolling hills and in the distance he saw tall rock formations rise up. Suddenly, the team veered from the road and quickened its speed as it rode through low scrub brush. Fargo saw the small cluster of buildings rise up.

The teams pulled into what was plainly a way station of a square building and two sheds. They instantly came to a halt alongside the long water trough as a man hurried from the building. Wearing trousers and a checkered vest, he halted as Fargo swung to the ground. He frowned from under thinning hair. "Who are you, mister?" he asked.

"Fargo. Skye Fargo," the Trailsman answered.

"Where's Willie Matson?" the man asked.

"He the usual driver?" Fargo returned.

"That's right," the man said.

"He wasn't with the stage. Neither were the passengers. It was a runaway all by itself," Fargo said. "I stopped it, let the horses find their way."

"What happened?" the man questioned.

"I don't know. Thought I'd get some answers here," Fargo said. "No driver, no passengers. You tell me."

"Jesus," the man said, staring at the coach. "This is only a way station, mister. You take the stage on to Bolton Flats. That's where it was headed."

"Bolton Flats?"

"Other side of those high rocks. There's a road through. You'll see it. Mr. Collins will want to see you. It's his stage line. I know he'll pay you for bringing it in," the man said.

Fargo thought for a moment. He didn't care a damn about pay for bringing in the wagon. But his curiosity was aroused. Besides, the quiet of his day had been thoroughly shattered. "All right, I'll take the stage in. Water the horses," he said and the man nodded almost eagerly. Fargo stepped into the house, found a tin pitcher of cool water, and refreshed himself. When he returned to the big Concord the horses had been rubbed down and watered.

"Collins. Buzz Collins," the man said. "The depot master will tell you where he is." Fargo nodded, climbed onto the coach, and sent it rolling forward. He set an easy pace for the team and finally reached the rocks and found a road leading between the towering stones. The road curved and climbed and soon Fargo found himself high into the rocks, mostly granite and basalt and honey-combed with narrow crevices on both sides of the road. The sound of the horses and the stage echoed through the stone canyons, obliterating all other noises. Fargo heard nothing until the shot exploded. He felt the sharp pain in his temple at the same instant. When he put a hand to his face he could feel the flow of red coursing down his cheek.

A wave of dizziness swept over him at once, sending the world into a spinning grayness. Fargo shook his head and winced in pain but the world returned, long enough for him to see the rifleman stop at one of the high rocks, then other horsemen coming out of the crevices toward him. He pulled on the reins to bring the stage to a halt as he felt himself toppling from the seat. Another shot rang out as he hit the ground. He gasped in pain as he lay half on his side on the gravelly road. He could see the figures moving toward him in a haze, wavy and indistinct, their voices faint. His eyes closed and he lay limp, hardly breathing, a line of red sliding down the side of his face from his temple. But he could still hear the faint voices.

"We got the damn stage," one voice said.

"No damn thanks to you," another voice said.

"How did I know they'd bolt?" the other voice said.

"Hell, you shot right next to them, you damn fool," the other said.

"What about him? He's dead," the first voice said.

"Throw him over the side," the other said. Fargo wanted to rise, turn, and kick out, but his body lay powerless, refusing to respond to his silent urgings, and his temple burned as if on fire. The dizziness stayed, closing out the world as he barely breathed. He felt himself lifted and flung into the air. He lost the last of his consciousness as he hit the first ledge, then the second. The world vanished completely. He was unaware of how many jutting rocks he struck as he fell, nor was he aware of finally hitting the bottom. He lay for uncounted, unknown hours, immersed in a void, without sound, sight, or sensation, dead so far as he knew, so far as anyone knew.

Then suddenly there was something. He didn't know what, but something, a flicker of awareness. Slowly, it took on substance and became more than a flicker. Awareness took on definition and became a cold hardness. Sensation. But the dead didn't feel anything. The dead didn't know sensation. They didn't reason, detect, come to conclusions. The dead weren't aware. He was alive, Fargo realized, the thought slowly sliding through him. A sound came from his throat, a strange, gargled sound. To Fargo it was laughter, wonderful, consuming laughter. He lay still, listening to the soft hiss of his breath and reveling in the sound. Finally, he tried moving the fingers of one hand, and felt them curl and tighten. He moved his arm next, stretched it out and followed with one leg, then the other, each movement an affirmation. He was alive. He pulled his eyelids open, blinked, and let his eyes adjust to the light and saw that the sun was still on the land. He slowly pushed to his feet, ignoring the pain that shot through his body, along the side of his temple.

But he knew he had been unconscious for hours. The dried state of the blood along his face told him that much. He peered up along the side of the rocks at the edge of the road high above. But the cliffside wasn't sheer, he saw. Ledges and clusters of uneven rock jutted out all over it. Wincing with the pain of bruised ribs and back, he began to pull himself up along the rocks. He moved slowly, gasping with each pull of his sore and strained muscles. It seemed to take forever before he reached the top and he had to stop often along the way. But finally he pulled himself over the edge of the road and lay there as he let his breath return. He pushed to one knee, whistled, waited, and whistled again and then again. When he heard the sound of hooves on the stone of the road, he rose to his feet and stretched out one arm as the Ovaro came around the curve.

He leaned against the warm strength of the great jet black neck for a moment and then ran his hands over the snow white midsection and jet hindquarters. "Give me up for lost, old friend?" he asked. "So did I." The horse shook his head and snorted in greeting and Fargo pulled himself into the saddle. The sun was sliding behind the distant peaks, and he let his thoughts begin to assemble what little he knew about the attackers. They had assumed the first shot had killed him and were in too much of a hurry to make sure. The fragments of their conversation swam back through his mind. Their chief concern had been the stage. They had stopped it someplace not that far away. Then the horses had bolted from a shot. Fargo let himself guess what had happened then. They'd been left with the passengers on their hands. They had to do something about them before they could take off after the stage. Tie and gag them? That'd take time. To shoot them would be faster. But they'd still have to drag the bodies out of sight.

Either way, they hadn't been able to immediately chase after the stage and the runaway team had continued its headlong flight. That's when he had first seen it, Fargo thought back. But one question hung in his thoughts. If they had stopped the stage to rob the passengers, why had they gone chasing after the coach at all? It didn't make sense. He couldn't come up with an answer to that but he had reconstructed a loose idea of what had happened before he'd first seen the runaway stage. His eyes went to the road and he saw that they had managed to turn the stage around. Wheelmarks showed they had taken the stage back the way it had come. He walked the Ovaro after the wheelmarks. Not only were there a lot of questions that needed answering, but perhaps people that needed rescuing. Besides, they had tried to kill him. He wasn't about to forget that.

Fargo followed the road back until it curved downward, leaving the high hills, and moving onto the flatland, where he circled the way station and rode up into the low hills, where he'd first seen the stage. He followed the wheelmarks and saw the road curve downward onto flatland heavy with forests of white fir interspersed with granite ridges. But the last of the day was sliding away, the blanket of night quickly rolling over the land. Trailing would be at an end in the dark and he found a spot between two large firs, unsaddled the Ovaro, and set out his bedroll. Before he stretched out, he used the water of his canteen to clean the caked blood from his temple and the side of his face. He ate a stick of dried beef from his saddle-bag and as he lay down, two questions continued to stab at him. Why had chasing after the stage been so damn important and what had happened to the passengers? The questions only went away when sleep came to shut them out.

He woke with the new day, his body less sore after a good night's sleep and he returned to tracking the wheel marks. He counted some six or so horses accompanying the stagecoach, but now, as he rode, he sought more than trail marks. His eyes scanned the terrain on both sides of the road, searching for trees pushed aside, brush disturbed, unnatural rock groups. But he saw nothing to investigate and the road grew more indistinct, becoming part of the land, where suddenly thick growths of serviceberry and dogwood emerged. A few hundred yards further, the trail marks were gone.

Frowning, Fargo swung from the saddle and proceeded on foot, the frown digging deeper into his brow. There were no wheel marks in the grama grass, no hoofprints nearby, nothing. The stage had disappeared. Only stages didn't just disappear. The trail had been covered up, carefully and expertly. No stage and, more importantly, no passengers. But they hadn't just vanished. They were somewhere, the passengers alive, he hoped, a grim hope, he admitted. Perhaps he could pick up signs, marks, a complete elimination of a trail was almost impossible. But they could have gone off in any direction. It would take too long to completely scour the land and he was growing fearful that time was important. He had to know more about the stage, where it had originated, about those who'd taken passage on it. Maybe then he'd have a chance to find the answers.

He turned the Ovaro around and put the horse into a fast trot. The stage was going to Bolton Flats. Maybe he'd find what he needed there. Maybe a waiting relative could help. Maybe Buzz Collins, owner of the stage line, could offer something. One thing was becoming terribly clear. It hadn't been an ordinary stagecoach holdup. Passengers were robbed, sometimes killed, in ordinary holdups. But the stages were left. They weren't chased down, then made to vanish. There was more here. But what and why? The questions rode with him as he drove the big Ovaro harder.

SIGNET

JON SHARPE'S WILD WEST

☐ **THE TRAILSMAN #147: DEATH TRAILS.** Skye Fargo was riding into double-barreled danger when he hit the trail in Texas teeming with murderous Mescalero Apaches and brutal *banditos*. He was out to settle the score with a trio of bushwhackers who had bashed in his head and stolen his roll. The only thing that the Trailsman could trust was his trigger finger in a crossfire where lies flew as thick as bullets and treachery was the name of the game. (178823—$3.50)

☐ **THE TRAILSMAN #148: CALIFORNIA QUARRY.** Sky Fargo had gone as far west and as deep into trouble as he could get on San Francisco's Barbary Coast. Now he was heading back east with a cargo of dead animals, a dodo of a professor, a stowaway pickpocket, and a beautiful fallen dove fleeing her gilded cage. Hunting them was Barbary Coast bully boy Deke Johnson and his gang of killers. (178831—$3.50)

☐ **THE TRAILSMAN #149: SPRINGFIELD SHARPSHOOTERS.** Skye Fargo could win most shoot-outs gun hands down—but this one was different. He was roped into a contest against the best in the West for a pile of cash that made the top gun worth its weight in gold. But when guns in the night started aiming at live targets, Fargo realized he had to do more than shoot to win, he had to shoot to kill . . . (178858—$3.50)

☐ **THE TRAILSMAN #150: SAVAGE GUNS.** Skye Fargo is caught in a wild Wyoming war in which he must fight for his life in a crossfire female fury, redskin rage, and the demented designs of a military madman who made war against the innocent and smeared his flag with bloody guilt. (178866—$3.50)

*Prices slightly higher in Canada

Buy them at your local bookstore or use this convenient coupon for ordering.

PENGUIN USA
P.O. Box 999 — Dept. #17108
Bergenfield, New Jersey 07621

Please send me the books I have checked above.
I am enclosing $_____ (please add $2.00 to cover postage and handling). Send check or money order (no cash or C.O.D.'s) or charge by Mastercard or VISA (with a $15.00 minimum). Prices and numbers are subject to change without notice.

Card #_____ Exp. Date _____
Signature_____
Name_____
Address_____
City _____ State _____ Zip Code _____

For faster service when ordering by credit card call **1-800-253-6476**

Allow a minimum of 4-6 weeks for delivery. This offer is subject to change without notice.